W9-AXO-632

the lifeguard

DEBORAH BLUMENTHAL

albert whitman & company
chicago, illinois

Library of Congress Cataloging-in-Publication Data

Blumenthal, Deborah.
The lifeguard / by Deborah Blumenthal.
p. cm.
Summary: Spending the summer at her aunt's beach house, teenaged Sirena struggles
with her parents' divorce and falls in love with a mysterious lifeguard.
ISBN 978-0-8075-4535-5
[1. Divorce—Fiction. 2. Love—Fiction.
3. Supernatural—Fiction. 4. Beaches—Fiction.] I. Title.
PZ7.B6267Li 2012
[Fic]—dc23
2011024771

The design is by Nick Tiemersma.
For more information about Albert Whitman & Company,
visit our web site at www.albertwhitman.com.

To Ralph

Prologue

**DANGEROUS RIP CURRENTS:
STAY OUT OF THE WATER.**

It was close to one hundred degrees, but swimmers were heeding the signs all along the beach. As far as the eye could see, no one was in the water.

Sirena wiped the sweat off her forehead with the back of her hand and stared out at the waves. For three days straight there was no relief from the steamy weather and the ocean stretched before her, cool, inviting, and off-limits. It was like someone putting a tall, icy glass of lemonade in your hand when you were thirsty, and then warning you not to drink it.

She waited until the lifeguard turned and walked to the far end of the beach. Slowly she got to her feet and made her way over the burning sand to the surf outside the swimming area in the direction of the jetty, carefully sidestepping blankets shaded with umbrellas and people pressing cold soda cans against their pink, flushed faces.

She wouldn't go more than a few yards from shore.

No deeper than her knees. She'd splash around and come right back. It would be safe. Anyway, when you were wet it was easier to tan, and her pale skin needed color.

She edged in, immediately aware of the drawing sensation around her feet as her red polished toenails sank beneath the gritty sand. The tingling pull of the water felt strange and exciting. She took a few baby steps farther until she were just above her ankles, aware of the water pulling as if it was trying to draw her out deeper. She smiled to herself —superwoman battling the brute force of nature—like the latest video game.

Only now there were no buttons to push.

No play. No pause. No stop.

No controls.

One more step forward and she dipped down to soak herself before getting out. But the water level deepened sharply as if she had stepped into a crater. She was thrown off balance as the water smacked against her with surprising ferocity. She tried to recover, to steady herself, but she toppled forward, thrown to her knees as the hard, pebbly sand abraded her skin. She tried to stand up again, but the current was like a powerful rope that lassoed her waist, tightening its chokehold, momentarily letting go then tightening again, intent on dragging her out farther and farther, deeper and deeper into the sea where no one could possibly find her or hear her calling, the wooden planks of the jetty now blocking out the light and striping her with shade.

She tried to grab hold to push herself out, searching frantically to see if anyone saw her or was running to help, but she saw nothing but the blank faces of people stretched out on beach towels, eyes closed, iPods blocking outside sound, oblivious to what was happening just a few hundred yards from their safe havens in the sand.

Her head bobbed to the surface momentarily and she pushed herself out from under the jetty, gasping for air, sheer terror spreading through her as she tried to lift an arm to signal for help. As if a strong, sadistic hand were above her, she was shoved roughly underwater. She panicked, running out of air, trying to hold her breath so she didn't swallow water. She surfaced again, gasping to fill her lungs, arms and legs flailing wildly, despite the leadenness and exhaustion overtaking her body, setting in like paralysis.

"HELP," she managed to shout before another wave crashed over her head, the pull of the riptide dragging her down again like a bouncing ball being roughhoused by the currents.

"HELP! HELP!" she cried over and over as her foot stomped on a hard mound in the sand. Without warning, the thing came alive, rearing up and viciously lashing her leg, sending a shock of searing pain through every nerve of her slackened body. As she sank to the silent, green world of the ocean floor, she opened her eyes and watched in horror as a swirling veil of blood surrounded her, darkening the water.

Dreaming.

She remembered dreaming.

A voice was whispering to her. "Breathe, breathe, breathe," it kept urging. A warm body was over hers, pressed against her. Someone bigger than she was, stronger, a powerful life force. A mouth on hers, warm lips, lips she didn't want to leave hers.

Then the dream ended.

She was left, abandoned.

Everything turned cold.

A deep, penetrating quiet filled the universe like a silent scream, just before the darkness.

one

The summer my parents were getting divorced in Texas, I was exiled. Like a child playing pin-the-tail-on-the-donkey, I felt blindfolded, turned in circles, then pushed to stumble off on my own.

I remember the airport. The roar of jet engines. The smell of diesel fuel. I headed for the plane with my beat-up carry-on bag that said Travel Pro—even though I wasn't one—my sketchbooks, art supplies, Ollie, my worn brown teddy bear, and a turkey sandwich on a roll, in case I didn't like plane food.

Before I boarded I stared up at the wide blue sky.

"Good-bye," I whispered. Then I waited. Would a cloud move or the sun shift? All I wanted was a sign, the smallest change, invisible to everyone but me. Something I could hold on to.

But there was nothing.

I fastened my seat belt and pulled it tight. We took off and I pressed my head back against the seat, feeling the rush as the plane went faster and faster and faster until it rose up into the air, as if it turned weightless. I reached up to the chain around my neck and closed my hand around the gold charm from Louisiana that my best friend, Marissa, gave me before I left.

"Arrive the same, leave different," it said.

Would it turn out that way?

⁓◦⊙◦⁓

Six hours later with a one-stop layover, I arrived on another planet.

Aunt Ellie was waiting for me at the small airport.

"Sirena," she said, hugging me.

I gave her a half smile and heaved my bag into the trunk of her Volvo wagon. She rolled down the windows, and we took off to her giant old gingerbread house near the water. She took my hand and I followed her up a flight of stairs to a dark attic bedroom. Dark until she flung open the blue wooden shutters.

"Voilà," she sang.

Sunlight lit the room like a flash fire.

I stepped to the window. Ocean everywhere with no beginning and no end. A view like that shrinks your head.

It puts your life into perspective.

"Surreal," I said.

For hours at a time that summer, I would sit on my window seat hypnotized by the waves, imagining the world hidden below the surface and wondering how I, a miniscule flicker of life, fit into the IMAX-sized universe before me.

My whole world would change after that summer. My parents were living together when I left. When I went back, they'd be apart.

"You'll come back to two homes instead of one," my mom tried. But a positive spin couldn't convince me I'd be gaining something, instead of losing everything. I have friends whose parents are divorced. They need calendars to tell them where to sleep and checklists to track down their stuff.

And then there were the holidays. Where would I go for Thanksgiving and Christmas? How could I celebrate? Who wanted to go back and forth between new homes, no homes? Who wanted to live with sad, single parents looking to start over?

What I wanted was for everything to stop and rewind. I wanted to live in before, not after.

But no one asked me what I wanted.

I try not to think of that now. Everything is different in Rhode Island. I guess that was the point of sending me.

Aunt Ellie's wooden house was built about a hundred

years ago, and when the wind blew it groaned like an old person getting out of a rickety chair. One night when it was stormy and it sounded like an atomic battlefield in the sky, I heard strange whispering coming from upstairs. Was I imagining things?

In Texas we have tropical storms and hurricanes that turn cars into boats. We have surprise tornadoes and roaches big as baby mice. But the one thing we never had, in our house at least, was ghosts.

"Is your house haunted?" I ask Aunt Ellie, pretending to joke.

She takes off her glasses and looks up momentarily from the National Geographic on her desk. "Oh sure," she says.

⸻❦⸻

My bedroom had blue-and-white wallpaper with old clipper ships with billowy sails and a double bed with a curvy white iron headboard and sheets as soft and white as magnolia blossoms. Fish X-rays in gossamer shades of inky blue hang on the walls like aquatic Warhols. But the best thing about the room is the pillow-covered window seat in front of the large bay window where I like to sit and watch the ocean.

I don't mind being away from home, I decide right then. I don't mind missing camp and being all alone.

In some ways I like it better, because no one will ask me questions I don't want to answer.

⁕

Aunt Ellie has a curly-haired dog named Will who's very curious about the new person in his house. He's part wheaten terrier, part something else. Like a dog detective, Will sniffs at my pants, and then at my hair when I bend down to pet him.

"Am I okay?"

His answer is to sniff and keep sniffing, instantly putting together a scent impression of me, the doggy equivalent of a police profile.

Will is five or so, Aunt Ellie thinks. She found him walking near the ocean one day, like a drifter who lost his way. He wasn't wearing a collar, and when she took him to the vet, he didn't have a microchip to tell them where home was. Even though he was a stray, he looked well-fed and he must have been well cared-for because he wasn't skittish in any way.

"It just seemed like the natural thing to bring him home and start the next chapter of his life and mine together," Aunt Ellie said. She already had three stray cats—Nina, Pinta, and Santa Maria—a gerbil, two turtles, and a canary, so one more animal wouldn't make all that much of a difference.

Aunt Ellie is like that. Nothing is a big deal to her. Not stray dogs or cats, not ghosts, not divorces, and especially not kids who are homeless. And that's good because I honestly don't think I could survive five minutes in her house if I felt that she pitied me or anything.

two

There won't be any structure to her summer," my dad
yelled to my mom when they were having one of the
fights they somehow assumed I couldn't hear. I sat in my
room helpless as a chicken facing slaughter. "What's she
going to *do* all day?"

My mom wasn't concerned about *doing*. She wasn't a
structure freak, or an ex-Marine, like my dad. "Ellie lives
at the *beach*," she said in a weary voice, like that should have
explained everything.

What she wanted most was to have me airlifted out of
our house, the city, and most of all, away from their fights.
The beach was a good alternative and probably their only
one. Without asking, I knew they wouldn't have money
anymore to send me to camp.

"Why can't I just stay home with you?" I asked my mom.

"It's hot here," was all she said. "I want you to have a real summer."

A nanosecond later I was gone.

Aunt Ellie seems okay with having me, although I can't imagine why. Maybe to her I'm some new specimen—the freaky teenage loser artifact—to study like a bug trapped in amber. Still, she's the relaxed type, independent. Totally not uptight. She's six years younger than my mom and she lives by her own rules, which is why she's content on her own in a creaky beach house with unmatched rattan furniture and weird specimens everywhere—from prickly cacti from the Sonoran desert to exotic seashells, Maori masks, and necklaces of snake vertebrae that seem to hiss a warning when you touch them.

I guess Aunt Ellie has so much life around her, she doesn't need a husband and kids, or maybe doesn't want them. I don't know because I never asked her.

"You don't ask unmarried people why they're not married because it's an embarrassing question, like why didn't you get asked to the prom," my mom once said, so I remembered that.

I'm relieved Aunt Ellie isn't married. If she was I'd have to deal with two people wondering what I'm thinking 24/7. The truth is more often I try not to, escaping to art or zoning to a safe haven in my head where it doesn't even matter if my parents are together or not.

"How do you split up someone's life?" I asked Marissa before I left. "Will my dad take my things from birth to eight, and my mom from eight to sixteen?" I was only half kidding. "Will the rest be dumped into garbage bags like clothes from a dead person and hauled off to a thrift shop?"

"You'll still be *you*," she said. "That's what counts. You won't change, you know?"

I didn't.

I didn't know anything. My brain was on mute along with my life. I'd walk into a room to get something, and then forget what it was. I'd stare into my closet unable to come up with a basis for picking one outfit over another, as if it actually mattered anyway. And when I opened the refrigerator or went to the grocery store, there was food everywhere, but nothing I wanted.

So why not move to a different state, even if it was the smallest of the fifty, a cubbyhole compared to Texas?

At least I'm in a house with a real animal. I fell for Will at first sight. He's sad and scruffy with liquid eyes and a Doberman-sized soul. But even though I'm dog-crazy, I'm almost glad we don't have a dog at home now because of a story I once heard. A married couple who had a dog they both loved desperately was splitting up. They were so angry with each other though that neither of them wanted to give the other the satisfaction of getting the dog.

The one who suffered most was the dog.

He ended up abandoned at a shelter.

⚬⟋⚭⟍⚬

Maybe Aunt Ellie knows things like that happen. Maybe that's why she never got married. Anyway, she seems to have this sixth sense about making people feel better, because before I arrived she bought me a present.

"Close your eyes," she said. When I opened them a wooden easel was open in front of me.

"I love it," I said. I really did. It was the perfect gift. It felt like someone had just crowned me a world-acclaimed artist. I never had an easel before and just looking at it made me feel important. I think she found it at a garage sale or something because it had little splatters of paint on it from the person who owned it before. Based on nothing, my turbo-charged imagination decided that the previous owner was an extraordinary painter who transferred mythical powers to the easel, and now it was my responsibility to uphold that artistic legacy. Of course if I told anyone something like that they'd just look at me and say, "You know, Sirena, you live in a total fantasy world."

And they'd be right.

Before I even unpacked my bag, I set up the easel near the window. I had never done any sea pictures before. I'd watch the water in different lights and changing weather to

10

know it and learn to draw it. I could do it, I decided, if I tried hard enough. All it would take was willpower.

<hr/>

What I didn't know then was that my entire summer at the ocean would be about knowing new worlds. Things would happen that weren't supposed to. Miracles would come true. And for the first time in my life, I would find out what it means to fall completely in love. Only it would happen in a way even *I* could never have imagined.

But let me start at the beginning.

three

My red bathing suit is old and faded. I haven't worked out in a month, so what I see in the mirror is the Pillsbury doughboy reincarnated as a 16-year-old girl. I could hide under a sweatshirt or wear a bathrobe to the beach, but rare-day alert: I don't care.

Why?

Refresher course: The state of big hair, big oil, shirts with snaps, and barbeque—my real world—is two thousand miles away.

Texas is also a state of man-made lakes and easy tides and hello, in front of me is a giant ocean with wild, crashing waves, so I morph into a psyched six-year-old and zigzag in and out of the water, playing tag with the surf. I pretend that Marissa's with me, because an imaginary friend is better than no friend at all. The sunlight glints off the water like a million winking lights.

"Ow," I call out, suddenly. Something sharp has stabbed my sole. Now I get why serious runners don't go barefoot. Pebbles and sharp shells poke out of the smooth blanket of wet sand. You can't avoid them. I hop into the water to numb the pain then focus on the music in my iPod and keep going.

I concentrate on the rhythm of the music; the bongo drum beats of my heart. Eyes closed, I'm making my way through a world of darkness, all outside distractions shut away. When one sense is closed off, do the others compensate? I open my eyes to make sure I'm not about to collide head-on with anyone, then close them again and fill my lungs with salty air.

Breathe, they tell you when you exercise. Don't forget to breathe. I take hungry breaths and fill my lungs, flashing back to early morning hikes at camp when the world smelled fresh and piney as if it were the first day of creation and it belonged to us alone, the children of paradise. We'd run back on empty chanting one sorry chorus of a hundred bottles of beer on the wall after another and finally reward ourselves by fueling up on spongy yellow French toast and maple syrup. Then we'd go back to the bunk to write letters, mostly because we wanted to get mail, the only tangible proof of popularity.

What if I really was blind? What would I pick up

through my other senses? I shut my eyes for longer, then I half-collide with an oncoming runner.

"Christ," he mutters under his breath.

He's pissed, I've broken his stride.

"Sorry," I mutter. When he's far behind me, I try again, this time with my headphones off. I listen to the squealing seagulls, breathe in the briny ocean scent, feel my skin tingle from the salty mist. I try to rise to another level of awareness and—

"WATCH OUT!"

"WHA—?"

I'm lifted up as if a twister swept me off the ground before I realize what's happening.

Only this was no force of nature.

Or if it was, it was disguised in a very human form. He moved fast, decisively, like a giant raptor lifting me off my feet. I see only tanned arms and long blond hair that smells like coconut.

"What are you *doing*?" I remember a self-defense maneuver and wrap my leg around his and kick him behind the knee. He loses balance, tumbling back into the sand. He doesn't let go so I plow into him and my chin slams a jaw bone as hard as a steer's horn.

"Ow," I moan, "what's *wrong* with you?"

He flips me in an instant and jumps up, lightning quick on his feet.

"Me?" He stares in disbelief.

I lay there for a moment, disoriented. *What just happened?*

The sun is at his back. His leans forward, casting a long shadow over me, like a giant web. That's when I see his face for the first time. I open my mouth, only no words come out.

Sun-striped hair falls straight against the sharp, smooth planes of a face, so classically perfect he could be a Greek statue come to life. Green-gold eyes hold mine a beat longer than they should.

I stare back.

And begin to unravel.

The corners of his mouth turn up. A slight headshake. "Did you think I was trying to *kidnap* you?"

"What *were* you doing?" A wave of annoyance rises up in me. "You scared me half to death." I get to my feet and brush the sand off my sore bottom. My face already throbs with pain.

He narrows his eyes and shakes his head dismissively, as if it's so obvious. "The *sea* urchin."

The *what*?

As if in answer, he lifts his chin in the direction of something in the sand, ahead of us. "You were about to *land* on it."

I stare at something black and scary, almost the size

of a tennis ball. It's covered with quills. He scoops it up and carries it back to me in his open palm like an offering. "They have sharp, venom-coated spines that break off in your skin," he says, almost in awe.

I step back and he leans toward me. "Not something you'd want to land on."

"Sorry...I...had no—"

He carries it to the water, then reaching back with the grace of a javelin thrower, he tosses it far out into the ocean. Without as much as a backward glance, the elite athlete sprints off in the opposite direction.

Only then do I see the back of his tank top:

LIFEGUARD.

four

I made sure to check the sign on the fence outside the beach: *Lifeguard schedule.* I had enough going on in my head without seeing his gloating expression when he saw me again—if he recognized me at all. I didn't tell Aunt Ellie what happened. She'd probably think it was funny and if she told her friend Mark, they'd both be convinced I was totally spacey.

But now Aunt Ellie wants to go walking on the beach. She's sun-phobic, so she only goes at sunrise or sunset.

"So wear sunblock."

"That doesn't *stop* the damage," she says. *It's obvious she's been over this before.* "It just slows it down. Anyway, I like the beach after everyone has gone home." She slips on prehistoric Keds and reaches for the straw hat hanging inside the door. "Want to come?"

Seven o'clock—he'd be off duty. I put on running shoes and go with her. The only people we pass on the beach are a woman asleep on a checkerboard towel and a couple under an apple-green umbrella with a sleeping baby book-ended between them. Will walks with us, every now and then stopping to sniff things on the beach. Aunt Ellie does that too, in her own way. Every so often she kneels down and unearths something like an archaeologist—a chunk of frosted sea glass, a glistening rock or an odd shell—then she holds it up to study it, deciding whether or not it has "the provenance"— she says with a small smile—to make it worth keeping.

Her prize shell, which she keeps in a black lacquer box on the coffee table, is called a spider scorpion shell. It's a twisted shell with a bumpy surface, mostly white with brown mottling. It's bigger than my entire open hand. But what makes it unusual isn't its large size. It has eight horny brown legs that extend outward, from top to bottom like twisted tentacles or an old person's crippled fingers. It looks like half sea shell, half sea monster.

"Kids find it scary," Aunt Ellie said when she saw me examining it.

"It reminds me of an expression we learned in French: *"Jolie laide."*

She nodded. "That's right. Pretty-ugly—something that's attractive despite its ugliness."

Something in the water catches Will's eye, or maybe his nose. He runs in searching for it, but when the waves come back in he darts out, as if he's afraid of their power.

"Do you swim, Aunt Ellie?

"Almost every morning, if the weather's good."

"I want to start swimming in the ocean, too."

I have to get over my nervousness about going out past the waves. I'm a decent swimmer now, it'll just take practice.

As we walk along I turn to Aunt Ellie. I don't know that much about her. What I remember most are the postcards she'd send us with foreign stamps from places around the world she visited, like Kathmandu, Jaipur, and Samos. I'd tack them to my bulletin board and then search the globe, pretending it was a board game and I had to figure out where in the world she was off to.

Now that we're out together, it's easier to ask her about herself.

"How come you don't work in an office like my mom?" She closes her eyes and shakes her head.

"Not the office type," she says. "I used to work as a nature teacher and talk to kids about different forms of life. We'd go on field trips to the park and I'd teach them about edible plants. I'd show them how to recognize scallions in the wild, rosemary, mint, all kinds of things," she says. "Then we'd make salad with the plants they learned about."

"I bet you could survive in the wilderness."

"I did, at least for a few days."

She took an Outward Bound trip, she says, and was part of a group that learned rock climbing and survival skills. Then everyone went off on their own to camp out in remote areas to test themselves.

I think about scorpions and snakes. "Weren't you scared?"

"At first and that's the point," she says. "But you learn to rely on yourself and it gives you a chance to discover your hidden strengths. If you're never challenged, you don't find out what you're capable of."

"I'd die of fear first."

"We surprise ourselves," she says.

⁓

As we walk, the giant apricot sun sinks lower in the dusty blue sky, like the world is a painting in motion. "I write books full-time at home now," she says. "I don't have to teach anymore because some of the science books did well."

"Just science books?"

"Science and lately science-fiction."

That reminds me of the ghost in the house. It didn't scare me, I was just curious. "So the...ghost... the one who whispers. Is that science or science fiction?"

A faint smile crosses her face. "Ah, good question."

But before she can answer, we run into Will, who's spotted something dead and rotting on the beach. He drops on top of it, rolling his back over it like he's doing an upside-down dance. It dawns on me that he'll bring the smell up to my room where he now sleeps.

"EEWW, Will, what are you *doing*?" He finally gets back on his feet and I throw water on his back to rinse off the dead, fishy smell.

Aunt Ellie shrugs. "It's the way he picks up the scent of his prey to hide his own scent," she says, "so if he goes hunting, they won't recognize him as an outsider...That's one theory, anyway. Another says rolling in vile stuff lets his pack know what he's found."

"He's the scent messenger."

"Sort of."

Since they learn about the world with their noses, that seems logical. I'm about to keep walking when Aunt Ellie suddenly crouches down and examines what Will rolled over. There's a concerned look on her face.

"What is it?"

"Hmmm," she says, almost to herself. "Strange." She lifts up a piece of what looks like a spear.

"What do you mean?"

She holds it out to show me. I reach for it, but she pulls it back. "It's sharp," she says. "Careful."

"What is it?" Very lightly I touch the ragged edge.

"It looks like a piece of the tail of a stingray, but you don't find them in these waters."

"So how did it get here?"

She shakes her head. "No idea."

We walk along and when I glance down at the sand by my feet I see something odd. It looks like a trail of droplets of blood. I lift my finger and that's when I see a razor-fine cut. *When did that happen? I didn't feel anything.* I put it in my mouth and suck on it, pressing hard, until finally, the bleeding stops.

⁓⊷⊶⊶⊷⁓

As we walk, the sun edges closer to the water until it's about to be swallowed up by the sea. A small boy kneels by the shore. He's playing with an inflatable snake. He hides it under the water, then jerks it out and shakes it in the face of his sister.

"Stop it," she shrieks. "Stop it."

He laughs at her, enjoying the game. "Baby," he says, taunting her. "Baby."

"Has there ever been a shark attack here?"

"A long time ago."

"What happened?"

"It was near sunset and the swimmer was close to shore." She scratches the back of her head. "We usually hear when there's a sighting in the area, but that time it happened out of the blue."

We walk along silently. Aunt Ellie looks like she's thinking about putting a scene like that into one of her books.

"Maybe if somebody had been watching closer, it could have been avoided."

"The lifeguards watch out all the time."

I work at keeping a straight face.

"And Antonio is usually out there. If anybody would have spotted it, it would have been him. He has this sixth sense."

"Antonio?"

"I forgot," Aunt Ellie says. "You haven't met him. He's a former fisherman. He was born in Brazil near the Amazon jungle. His father was a doctor, but he's lived here for most of his life. Ever since he retired and sold his boat, he spends most of the day on the beach, painting. A gallery in town sells some of his work."

"I'd like to meet him."

"I'm sure he'd like to meet you. He's eighty and still very handsome," she says. "And he has a weakness for pretty blue-eyed blondes."

five

The beach is off-limits.

I drift around town and down double lattes at a
coffee bar until I'm bug-eyed. I look at houses and gardens
trying to imagine living in my dream home with my dream
boyfriend. I stare into cars to see what people leave behind
inviting break-ins; buy camouflage printed flip-flops as if
there's a reason to, and then beaded bracelets made by eight-
year-olds who sit on the street with a pathetic, crayoned For
Sale sign; and end up on a swing in the playground for so
long that the local mothers must be convinced I'm a victim
of arrested development.

If Aunt Ellie thinks it's strange that I haven't gone
near the water, she doesn't say. But one week goes by and
another begins and hel-*lo*, why am I punishing myself?

Girl with closed eyes who almost landed on a sea urchin sentences herself to beach ban and total boredom.

Head check. He was the one who wrenched me off the ground. Was I supposed to know what he was doing? I mean a *sea urchin*? That has to be rare. How do I know he didn't plant it there, like boys in school who think it's amusing to wait until girls go to the bathroom and then leave dead bugs on their seats to gross them out. Maybe he enjoys freaking girls out, or has some sick need to play savior, like firemen who start fires.

Whatever. It was time to move on. By now he had to have forgotten the whole thing—and me. Girls probably did stupid things around him all the time to turn his head.

So I go.

Blanket, sketchbook, pencils, sunblock, and lip gloss, all in a backpack slung over one shoulder. Overcast sky, no blinding brightness. Easier to work. There are fewer people than usual on the beach and I stake my ground.

Then I glance up.

The lifeguard chair is empty, so maybe it's his day off. Whoever has taken his place must be off somewhere. I'm relieved, I can't help it. I settle in the swimming area, far to the side of his chair, spreading out Aunt Ellie's pink Balinese blanket. I prop my sketchbook against my bent legs and start sketching. The whole beach is my figure modeling class and I'm obsessed with drawing all the different poses. Bent legs, half-buried feet. Arms shielding eyes. I fill page after page. What I want is to draw figures that breathe—that look alive, like they could get up off the page and move—not flat, lifeless caricatures. The quickest way to judge how good an artist is is to look at his figures.

Only what I hate is when you work harder and harder on something, and the more you try, the worse it comes out. I see now that what I've done is total and complete junk. One by one I rip out the pages and crumple them up, hiding the evidence in my bag.

I need a break. Sweat is prickling my underarms so I get up and head for the water. Then I turn back and cover my arms and legs with sunblock and dot my forehead. When I'm tan my eyes look bluer, my hair lighter.

Thunderstorms are predicted later in the day so the water's rougher than usual. The waves crash against me, the trespasser, trying to shove me out of the water, but I stand my ground easing in. I go in waist-high at first, then deeper, just past where the waves break. I bob up and down, like an inflatable ball and I relax. You can do it, I tell myself.

I start to make my way back to shore, but my arms ache. I lie back letting the water carry me like a baby in a giant swing.

Flashback to summers with my parents on the beach, one on either side of me, holding my hands. They'd pull me up when the waves came, airlifting me from harm. I miss that, I miss them. Will I ever get over that? Now all

I have is a voice in my head that warns me to go back. No mother, only Mother Nature, and what does she care?

A whistle blows. It blows again harder and longer. Someone is farther out than I am. The warning is for him. Hands motion for him to come back in. Instinctively I swim toward shore too, taking deep breaths and swimming parallel to the surf until I'm in shallow water. I run back to the blanket. As I lean over to pick up my towel I look up.

My eyes are drawn to the lifeguard station like the tides to the pull of the moon.

And there he is.

Male centerfold.

Perfect as a retouched photo, only there's nothing about him that needs to be airbrushed or altered in any way. Nothing to erase, hide, or even improve on, no matter how gifted the artist. He's flawless.

He rests back easily against the chair, one leg bent for support. Within arm's reach is a surfboard, a rescue buoy, and a first-aid kit.

Ready to save a life.

What would it feel like to be pulled in by him? To be tethered to him by his rescue buoy, or next to him on the surf board? S-O-S, I want to shout. A smile rises in my throat. Good thing he can't hear my head.

I watch him watch the beach through binoculars; a baseball cap shades his face. A black leather cuff is wrapped around his wrist. He's ripped, yet as lean as a long-distance runner. I want to draw him, I want to get him down on paper to study, to know. I glance around, surprised that any eyes are closed. Are they all blind?

He lowers the binoculars for a few seconds to wipe his forehead with the back of his hand and I study him face forward, struck again with how fiercely beautiful he is. The straight, narrow nose, the finely angled bone structure. An artist's model of perfect proportions. He looks wary, self-absorbed. I try to imagine how his face would change if he laughed, or at least smiled. I don't imagine that comes easy to him.

Do you see me studying you?

As if in answer, he lifts the binoculars and peers through them in my direction. There's no one else in his line of sight.

I don't care anymore about being embarrassed.

I don't care what happened before.

I stare and keep staring, not drawing as much as a breath as the world stops and time seems suspended and everyone and everything recedes into absolute nothingness.

Except us, taking each other in.

Neither of us moves.

Perspiration beads on my face and upper lip in the fiery heat. A droplet breaks free and trickles down the side of my face, stinging the corner of my eye. I blink, ignoring it.

I won't look away first. My heart beats so hard that it hurts.

He doesn't move.

I lift my chin and wait.

So does he.

I hold my ground. A silent challenge.

I'm going to win.

He turns sharply, sweeping his glance over the rest of the broad swath of beach.

And the game is over.

For now.

I release a breath I wasn't aware I was holding and turn away, sinking onto the soft blanket facing the water, the sun branding my back.

I lecture myself as I decompress.

Push emotion aside, Sirena. Go for cold logic and clear reason. He's a reclusive cat with a monstrous ego. Anyone can see it in the way he carries himself, in the way his eyes X-rayed my head, my heart. Poseidon, Greek god of the sea, shaker of the earth, drawing women with his power and allure.

Welcome to my B movie.

It's infantile to play games, I decide right then. I want nothing more to do with him. Why would I sign on for a summer of hero-worship and disappointment?

You'd have to be crazy.

six

D o you have a boyfriend?"
Aunt Ellie smiles slightly and tilts her head left and then right, like half yes, half no.

Yes, Mark is a boy, actually a man. He's even hot for forty-five or so. And he's her friend. In my mind that equals *boy-friend*. He lives in the next town and owns a seafood restaurant where everyone goes for the lobsters and fried clams packed into cardboard containers like Chinese food. Aunt Ellie is such a fan of the food, she says, that Mark joked he'd have to either make her a partner or start taking her out.

"Mark moved to Rhode Island after his wife died," she says. "He lived on Cape Cod before, so Rhode Island wasn't a *big* change, just a change, and he needed to be someplace else."

Maybe I identify with that.

Right away I feel for him and like him. Mondays the restaurant is closed so Mark comes over. He drives a red vintage pickup truck with the fish logo of the restaurant on the door. He walks in carrying fish wrapped in brown paper.

I remember seeing a real fish for the first time in the grocery store. "MAAAA, IT HAS EYES," I shrieked. My mom just laughed. But how was I supposed to know? We didn't live near the water.

Mark heads for the kitchen to cook dinner. "Without work," he says, with a smile, "I'm like a fish out of water."

Aunt Ellie is happy to give him the job. She opens white wine and washes a bunch of spinach as big as a bouquet. Mark does everything else. It's like a Food Channel ballet the way he moves, first reaching for the lemon juice, the soy sauce, then chopping the garlic and the ginger with short, precise strokes using his own knife. Without raising his head, he glances up and watches me watching him. He enjoys the audience, I think, but he's cool. He doesn't say anything.

Mark doesn't use measuring spoons like my mom; he just seems to know how long to shake each of the bottles lined up on the counter. I remember one of my vocab words—intuitive. You just know things, it means.

Even when he isn't smiling, Mark's face looks amused.

His dark mustache curls around the corners of his mouth and his brown eyes are surrounded by squint lines, probably because he uses his eyes so much when he smiles. He wears jeans and a blue work shirt with the sleeves rolled up. On the breast pocket in red stitching it says, "The Shack." If he didn't own a restaurant, Mark would be a fireman, I think. If someone was in trouble, he's the type who would be there to help.

Which makes me think of the ghosts again. Did Aunt Ellie ever talk to him about them? I could imagine both of them going upstairs with a flashlight like amateur detectives. I don't bring that up though because they'd laugh at me for being spooked.

When he finishes mixing everything together just right, he pours it over the fish and covers the container. He flips it over so both sides get equal time in the saucy bath. He sets it aside to soak, then turns to me.

"So you like it here?"

"I like it…It's just so different from Texas."

"I was there once," Mark says. "Saw a rodeo, ate barbecue. We even drove down to Padre Island and went to the beach." He grins. "It's a lot hotter than Rhode Island."

Something in my face must tell him what I'm thinking. He crosses his arms over his chest and leans across the kitchen counter toward me

"Life changes, Sirena," he says, his husky voice almost

hoarse, "and you can't help it. But your life isn't over when your parents divorce."

I shrug.

He tilts his head to the side. "How old are you?"

"Almost seventeen."

"You'll be moving out in a year or so when you go to college."

I nod.

"And what they're going through doesn't change the fact that they love you. In fact, they'll both need you more."

I try to stop my eyes from tearing up. "I know." It comes out haltingly, breathy. I can't help it. It's easier to let your feelings out with some people more than others, and Mark listens with his heart.

"Don't spend time feeling sorry for yourself," he says, rubbing the back of his neck. He stares into the distance as though thoughts of his own life tug at him. Abruptly he turns back to me. "Think about the good things ahead of you."

"Like what?"

He opens a white box on the counter and slides it over to me. Inside there's a chocolate cake with a red candy lobster on top. He scoops chocolate frosting onto his finger and dabs it on the tip of my nose.

"Like dessert."

seven

My mom calls every other day. "Hi baby, how are you doing?"

I avoid feelings and go with activities: Drawing, walking, eating. I tell her about Mark and his cooking, his restaurant. Lobster, clams, good things.

"Does Ellie like him?"

Where is she heading with this? "I don't know, Mom." I exhale hard.

"I mean, you know, as a boyfriend."

"They're friends...I can't tell. God, what's the difference?"

That gets me thinking about my mom and other men. Are there any others? I never met any. There was only my dad until now. Would she start going out again?

Is there anything grosser than thinking of your mom or dad in bed with someone else? I remember asking Marissa.

"What about them doing it with *each other*?" She laughed. "*That* isn't gross?

Only my parents probably weren't doing it—with each other anyway. I stop my head from going there. Too raw.

Anyway, I refuse to meet their new girlfriends or boyfriends. I won't be home if they bring them over. I'll sleep someplace else, even the back of the car if I have to.

New subject. "What's happening with the house?"

"I think we finally found a buyer," she says, "but we haven't closed yet. It'll take a couple of months."

"Months?"

"It's a long process."

"And then?"

"We're both looking at places. Prices are crazy...it's going to be a while."

Silence. We're both just holding on, breathing on the life line between us.

"I'm glad you're in a prettier place," she says, finally.

The beach or my state of mind?

"I miss you," she adds.

"I miss you, too," I say, finally.

"Are you all right up there?"

Is she going to cry? "I'm fine," I say, the parent reassuring the nervous child.

Aunt Ellie goes to the grocery store for dinner, so Will and I walk to the beach. There's a leash law, at least that's what the rusted metal sign on the fence says, among other things.

No alcohol
No loud radios
No spitting
No glass bottles
No ball playing
Dogs on leashes

I've seen other dogs running on their own so I let Will off the leash and he bolts. I have a whistle in my pocket that Aunt Ellie says brings him back if he goes too far. Will is in better shape than I am and he races along like a thoroughbred. He's having the time of his life running free in the powdery sand, digging holes and then skipping back and forth in and out of the water, as if he's in tune with its power and mystery on his special dog frequency. After a few minutes of trying to keep up with him, I slow to a walk.

Somewhere behind me a whistle blows. I look out to see if a swimmer went out too far, but I don't see anyone. It blows again. Will pivots and starts running back toward me. To him it's a command.

"Good boy, Will," I call out. I raise my hand and wave to show him where I am, Only when he gets closer, he doesn't run up to me. He heads up toward—no.

The lifeguard.

Obediently he kneels at his feet, head raised.

*WILL! How could you do this to me? This is the last time I am
ever letting you off the leash.*

I suck in all the oxygen I can hold and head over to get
him. I glance at the lifeguard and then look away. "Sorry," I
blurt out. That seems to be the operative word around him.

He stands there silently, one hand rubbing the back
of his neck. His eyes embarrass me, that unswerving gaze.
Does he even blink?

"C'mere Will." I fumble, suddenly totally
uncoordinated, trying to attach the stubborn clip of the
leash to the ring on his collar as he edges away to avoid it.
Coordination 101 and I'm failing. No chance of a genius
grant.

"What?" I shoot back. He's still staring.

I look away, and then glance up at him again after
I manage to pry the clip open. I won't bring up what
happened. What would be the point?

I want to be cool, detached. This is so not a big deal.
But it's impossible to look away. I'm drawn to him as though
a magnetic field surrounds him. It isn't something I can get
past and I'm filled with wonder again the way I was the first
time I saw him. He must know that. How could he not?
Everyone around him has to feel fatally flawed. Could that
not go to your head?

What I want most is to stop and objectively study his
face to isolate what it is exactly that makes him so rarified.

Two eyes, a nose and a mouth—same as every other member of the entire human race. Only nothing about him adds up logically. He's got an aesthetic edge. He isn't *like* anyone else and it eats at me. I'm surprised he doesn't walk on water. Instinctively, I resist the power and sway he holds over me.

He crouches down and scratches Will's head, then lifts his eyes up to me. "There's a leash law on the beach, Sirena," he says, softly.

How does he know my name?

"But nobody really follows it, do they?"

He rises to his feet and lifts his chin slightly. "When I'm on duty they do."

"Why can't Will run free? He isn't bothering anybody."

He shrugs. "Not every dog is as friendly as Ellie's."

"Has there ever been a problem?"

He shakes his head back and forth slowly. "Not while I'm on duty."

I ignore that and start to lead Will away.

"How's your face?" he asks, reeling me in.

I stop and turn back to him. Instinctively, I rub it. "Still bruised."

He steps toward me and studies the side of my face, reaching out and slowly running his fingers lightly up and down the side of my jaw, his eyes grazing my lips.

38

"Still swollen," he says, almost to himself.

A caring gesture, showing concern, nothing more. Only my body registers it as something else entirely. I resist the urge to take the one small step that would close the space between us. I look away momentarily and try to stifle a laugh that's lodged in my throat because the idea is so absurd and out of the question.

Does he see what he's done to me? Feel it?

How can he not?

I'm suspended, as transparent and brainless as an undulating jellyfish in its watery skin, reduced to feeling and sensing, floating along without thinking.

What do I say or do?

I want to grab Will's leash and run somewhere quiet to sit alone and collect my thoughts and go over what really happened, what it meant.

Or didn't mean.

All the touchstones of normalcy, familiarity, and sanity have vanished. I've lost my center of gravity, sinking into a vortex of helpless longing like a pathetic adolescent with an aching, clichéd crush.

Does his face say I'm imagining this?

It's stoically expressionless, giving nothing away. What did I expect? He isn't short of breath. He's ethereally calm, controlled, supremely confident, guarding the intimate thoughts in his head, and I am so totally out of my league with him. His face reveals the mildest curiosity, if anything.

"What about you?" says some other, sure-of-herself me who magically appears to rise to the challenge. My hand reaches up and strokes the side of his jaw.

Is he real? I need to touch his perfect skin and find out what he feels like. My fingers lightly caress the spot where I landed on him. His skin isn't warm, it's hot, as if the heat of the sun is inside him.

"Here, right?"

A corner of his mouth curls up slightly. There's the slightest flicker in his cool, green eyes. He shakes his head from side to side. "I don't bruise," he says, dismissively. His eyes offer a silent challenge to figure him out.

I cock my head to the side, not understanding. "What do you mean you don't bruise?"

He shrugs. "It's never happened."

If he was human he'd have skin and blood and being slammed in the face ruptures blood vessels and causes bleeding and bruising, at least that's what I learned in biology and I got an A. No one ever said any of that was up for discussion.

What do I say to that?

I stand there awkwardly, the silence widening, creating a larger and larger divide between us. Unintentionally, I sigh and look at him questioningly, instantly sorry I've given him even a hint of a reaction. He smiles slightly, enjoying putting me on edge, it's so clear. I hate that. This time he holds my gaze.

Now *he's* determined to win the staring contest.

Only alpha-dog Will comes to my rescue, breaking the impasse, convincing me he's not only smart, he's brilliant. He totally gets it. He jumps up on me and barks. It's time to take him home and feed him. He knows in his bones when it's supper time and his animal alarm clock has gone off. I start to lead him away.

"Well, then, you're more than a lifeguard," says that voice in me from I don't know where. "You're Superman."

He shakes his head back and forth slowly. "I can't fly," he says, raising an eyebrow. "At least, not yet."

I stand there and stare for another moment, and that sets Will off again.

"He's jealous," he says, amused.

I shrug. "Probably just hungry."

He smiles slightly. It doesn't derail him. Not the least hint that he felt the slight.

I lead Will away, waving with the tips of my fingers. "Bye, Superman."

eight

Black storm clouds hover over the beach, like dark smudges on a white page, darkening the silvery afternoon sky. Spiky waves crash over the sand where just the day before, bathers sat in the warm sun before a calm ocean.

Aunt Ellie stays inside working, sipping homemade ginger tea from a red mug she probably made in a pottery class. Her new book is on pterodactyls. I glance over her shoulder at an article she's reading. Their wing spans ranged from twenty to thirty inches to over forty feet.

"As big as a plane!"

She smiles. "And particularly scary because they had sharp eyes." She points to a picture. "Imagine him swooping down searching for prey."

"Are you writing fiction or nonfiction?"

"I haven't decided. I have to see where it goes."

I read in the living room for most of the afternoon, but Will needs to go out so I volunteer. As we pass the lifeguard's chair I glance up, half expecting to see him there in spite of the oncoming storm: lord of the beach watching over his domain.

But the chair is empty.

I unclip Will's leash and let him run free.

What does a lifeguard do on his days off? I don't see him hunched over Facebook reaching out to friends. He doesn't seem like the type to have twelve hundred of them—not that he wouldn't if he posted his picture. I can't imagine what type he is at all. He isn't like anyone I've ever met before. I climb up the side of the chair and sit in his seat to view the world from up high. I want to see the world through his eyes, and know what it feels like to be him. I look around. Did he leave anything behind that will give me hints about who he is?

Nothing.

And everything.

A dark blue plastic bottle. Sunblock, SPF 45. I unscrew the top and I'm flooded with his sweet, enticing scent—coconut, citrus, and jasmine. I cup my hand and fill it with the milky lotion, rubbing it into my face and neck.

Now I'm like Will who rolls on things to absorb their

smell. I'm cloaked in his perfume, his essence, so as I stalk my prey I won't be seen as an outsider. I place the bottle back where I found it and make my way down the side of the chair. *His* chair.

I examine the chipped, white weathered wood like a scientist who studies tree rings to learn about past events in history and changes in the climate. Only this chair isn't parting with its secrets. It's as inscrutable as he is, high above the ground, confronting the water. It reminds me of a still life about natural forces and isolation. The chair is the only clue of humanity. Like Aunt Ellie's house, does it have ghosts? What kind of stories would they tell?

Will barks at me. He's jealous of whatever has stolen my attention. I take a tennis ball out of my pocket and throw it. He runs for it and then races back to me, dropping it at my feet. I toss it again and again. Will never tires of the game. Just to see what he does, I flip over and walk on my hands. I've studied gymnastics since kindergarten after my mom took me to the circus. I watched acrobats walking on their hands and doing flips and I came home determined to do it too.

Will cocks his head to the side.

"You're not the first one who doesn't know what to make of me." I keep walking on my hands, studying the world turned upside down—the way it feels to me.

The sky darkens as we start to walk home. I hear distant thunder and walk faster, ready to break into a run. Will inhales something in the wind and then hurries along with me. He senses danger and doesn't want to get caught either. Moments later there's a deafening clap of thunder. In minutes the heavens come down and we break into a run. A wall of water washes over me and I look as though I've been swimming in my clothes. Will turns into a drowned rat and I look at him and start to laugh. He tries to shake the water off his head so he can see, but he realizes how futile it is. We start to cross the street, but it's nearly impossible to make out whether any cars are coming because everything is shrouded in fog and my eyes are being washed with rain.

But off in the distance, I make out a yellow haze. Very slowly it becomes brighter. The glow of headlights, I realize, as a car approaches slowly and cautiously. It looks like it's going to pass us, but it stops. The window on the passenger side rolls down.

"Get in, I'll give you a ride."

Does he patrol the beach by car when he's not on duty?

Without hesitating, I pull open the door and get into the front seat. Will bolts into my lap. The side window closes and the air inside the car becomes as heated and heavy as the night air in Houston.

I inhale his sweet smell of jasmine, citrus and coconut—it must be in his blood by now. Water drips from my hair, soaking the seat. Will shakes his whole body, showering both of us, and nervous laughter bursts out of me uncontrollably. I feel wired, my pulsating blood buzzing in my head.

"Are you sure you want us in your car like this?

His face breaks into a half smile. "I'm not afraid of water." He reaches into the back seat and hands me a towel and I begin to dry my hair, He glances over at me once, then a second time. I watch him back with the odd feeling that drying my hair has assumed some greater meaning and significance.

"So what do you do when you're not saving people?" I say to fill the awkwardness.

"That's…more than a full-time job."

"Thanks for picking us up. I thought we'd have to swim home." I start to laugh again for no reason. If he thinks I'm insanely crazy, he doesn't show it. To do something with my hands, I take the towel and blot the water off the front seat. I steal glances at him as he drives, his left hand on the wheel, the right lightly resting on the worn jeans covering his thigh, fingers spread slightly apart. Like a video camera, my eyes record every last detail and imprint it all on my brain's hard drive. I absorb every bit of information I can from studying him, as if seeing him up close will let me understand who he is and what's in his head.

Every part of him is impossibly perfect. The strong shoulders. The swell of his biceps, half hidden by the soft edge of his white T-shirt. The lean forearms lightly covered with blond hair. Long, slender fingers. Smooth, even nails cut short and rounded. I fight the urge to reach out and feel his skin.

The car stops suddenly, the engine dies. Where are we? I look up surprised as if I'm being awakened from a dream. In front of Aunt Ellie's. Already?

I don't want to leave.

We sit for a moment without talking, mesmerized by the deafening downpour. Will's wet, doggy smell competes with the coconut and jasmine, like reality at odds with fantasy. In the warm, moist space of the car my senses feel overloaded.

He leans his head back and stares at the windshield. "Like being inside the car wash," he says.

It's almost impossible to see out. I drop my eyes to the idiotic orange poop bag wrapped around the handle of the leash, like a scarf around the strap of a designer bag. The rain pounds like hail on the roof of the car. Everything ordinary now vibrates with extrasensory significance—what it must be like to be high on acid. What is it about being next to him that does that? Every breath I take feels super-saturated with energy and oxygen, making me jittery and on

47

edge. Does that happen to everyone around him, or is it just me?

"Do you want to come in for a soda or something?" I come up with, breaking the silence. "Just to get out of this?" It's lame, I can't help it.

He smiles. "I have to take off, but thanks."

"Thanks for the ride."

"Stay safe," he says.

We dash from the car and his eyes are on me—I can feel them. And then for the first time, it occurs to me.

I don't even know his name.

⌁⌁⌁

Will and I race into the house and I go upstairs to change, slipping into a dry T-shirt and shorts. I sit on the edge of my bed and replay what just happened.

There's no way he would have come in. No way. What was I thinking, that he'd want milk and cookies and we'd hang out and watch TV or play video games like sixth graders?

I shouldn't have asked him. I should have just shut up and acted cool. Now I feel stupid.

What else is new?

We have soup for dinner. Aunt Ellie's pot of clam chowder could feed twenty. After we eat I go upstairs and turn on the TV. She never watches so she doesn't have the cable stations we have at home. For lack of anything better, I sit through a rerun of *Friends*. My head is back on the pillow and my eyelids start to flutter.

That's when I begin to hear them.

Strange sounds. At first I think they're part of my dreams.

Only they're not.

I sit up totally awake now, but they don't stop. They're eerie. Not animal, not human, moaning and then a disturbing higher frequency whistling. It sounds like the howling the wind makes when there's a tropical storm so fierce the window frames whine and you can feel the vibrations in your bones, like scratching on a blackboard.

Only now it's not the wind.

It's something supernatural and less benign.

Only what?

I lean forward and turn down the TV. The sounds seem to stop. I ease the volume back up and it starts again. Will is next to me on the bed. I can swear he's lifting his ears up straight as though he hears it too. Then I spot Nina, the most docile of Aunt Ellie's cats. She's curled up in the corner, eyes wide and shocked, shining like glass marbles. Is it my imagination, or does she look spooked too?

I hold my breath. Is someone or something playing with me? Or does it just feel safer, protected, when other house sounds muffle it?

"It's freaky, right, Will?"

His ears shoot straight up again on high alert, but he hasn't processed what it is. He cocks his head slightly as if he's picking up something curious out of human range. I leave the TV on and edge toward the staircase. Will bolts after me.

"Aunt Ellie?" I break into a run down to her office, yelling out to fill the air with the reassuring sound of my own normal voice and presence.

She looks up, concerned. "What is it, Sirena?"

"Can I ask you something?"

She leans back in her chair and swivels around to face me. "Shoot."

"I'm hearing these...sounds... from upstairs."

She reaches a hand up to the side of her jaw and rubs it, nodding.

"Do you know what..."

She nods knowingly again.

"Are they always the same?"

She takes her glasses off. "Not always, why?"

"Do you think the ghost is trying to tell us something?"

Her face softens. "I don't know if it's true or not, but there's a story about a woman who lived in this house. Her husband had a fishing boat, I heard. Supposedly one day he went out to sea and never came back. Nobody ever found him or the boat so the story people started telling was that the voice was his wife's and she was crying out for him. They said she'd never stop until she found him."

"When do you hear it?"

"When the weather's bad…They say he left when there was a bad storm approaching."

"Do you believe that?"

"I can't *not* believe it, even though I'd be hard-pressed to find concrete evidence."

I feel an icy draft on my neck at that moment. But how is that possible? The house isn't air conditioned and it's hot outside. Is it my imagination? Tiny goose bumps suddenly rise up and dot my arms. Aunt Ellie watches as I rub my hands up and down my arms to warm myself. "Is it cold in here?"

She shakes her head. "That happens to me sometimes, too."

"Omigod."

The chill finally passes and I try to take a deep breath. "Have you ever seen…*it*?"

She makes a face as if to say, hmmm, that's a hard one. "I haven't actually seen what comic books show you ghosts look like, but once or twice at night, when it was raining hard, I thought I saw a white light, or something like that scoot down the hallway."

"Did it scare you?"

"The first time, a little, but now, no…I feel sorry for

her in a way, so I'm glad I can share my house with her—or that she lets *me* share *her* house."

"You're so cool about it. If my mom were here she'd run from the house screaming."

"I've come to accept that there are things about this world that we'll never nail down...never know about for certain. And in some ways I enjoy the mysteries—and the possibilities. But I do believe there are different kinds of life and spirits or ghosts, or whatever you want to call them. But—" She stops and her face softens, "fortunately we seem to share our little universe with gentle ghosts, so no, I don't worry about it too much."

I hold that thought as Will and I climb back upstairs. I can't help thinking of a story I read in the local paper, just before Halloween, about a real haunted house that was supposedly built on the site of an old cemetery. There was a place in the backyard where the owners of the house insisted that their dog refused to go. One day when the police came to the house to investigate, they brought cadaver dogs. They immediately went to that exact spot and stood right there like they knew bodies were buried below. And inside the house, all kinds of creepy, unexplained things used to happen. Lights went on by themselves, so did the TV and the water faucets. Upstairs, doors shut when no one was there. And even though the owners' dog wasn't white, there were white dog hairs around the house. A white dog had lived in the house, but it was many years before.

The scariest thing of all, though, was the picture of the upstairs bathroom the local newspaper took and used with the story. If you looked at it closely, you could actually make out the evil-looking face of a man with dark, piercing eyes.

Only the bathroom wall was bare. There were no picture of any kind on it, and no one at all could identify the mysterious image that appeared for the world to see.

"Do you decorate your house with spooky lights or decorations for Halloween?" the reporter jokingly asked the owners.

"No," they said. "To us it isn't funny."

The wife took pictures in the house and when she looked at them she could see little white disks she called orbs, floating in the air. They resembled tiny flying saucers.

I open my bureau drawer and take out my camera. I snap pictures of one part of my room and then the other.

Click. Click. Click. Click.

Then I look at the pictures, examining them carefully. Nothing.

I exhale, relieved, and toss the camera aside. I lay in bed studying the pictures. A few minutes later, I pick up the camera again and shoot more pictures.

Click. Click. Click. Click.

I walk to the edge of the bed and turn on the other lamp. I sit down and study the pictures again in the brightness.

And that's when I see them.

The faint, white circles.

They're everywhere.

nine

"There are *ghosts* in the house here," I whisper into the phone to my dad.

"What?"

"GHOSTS."

Ghosts?" he says, a smile in his voice. "Okaaaay."

He thinks I'm teasing. "I'm not kidding, dad."

"How do you know?"

"Because when it rains or storms they come out, they come out in the attic, where I have my bed."

Silence.

My dad is now weirded out. He doesn't know what to say. He's not the kind of guy who believes in ghosts, and even if he did I don't think he'd be spooked by them, at least at first. Reality is more than enough for him to cope with. But even if there were ghosts where he slept, he'd probably fall dead asleep so fast that he'd be oblivious to them if they came out—either that, or his snoring would scare them off.

"Ghosts like Casper or what?" he blurts out.

"White, weird, shadowy, I don't know exactly."

"Did you tell Aunt Ellie?"

"Of course *she* knows, it's her house," I tell him.

"Yeah, sure." Another pause. "Does it scare you or what?"

"Yes...and no."

"So, switch beds with Ellie when it storms. Ask her to bunk with the damn ghosts."

"It's not that they're unfriendly or dangerous, it's just...you know, so weird."

"Life is weird, baby. You have to get used to it."

ten

PMS is up there with ghosts in turning you into someone you don't want to be. I'm stretched out on the living room couch, down and dirty in boxers and a sleep shirt. If I were home on the weekend during the school year, the scene might go:

My mom: "Sirena, for God's sake get dressed."

Me: "I'm studying for a stupid test. Why do I have to get dressed?" I'd slam the door of my room and go back to studying, Facebook, and ice cream.

Only not here.

Aunt Ellie's had her fill. She plants herself in front of me, hands on hips. "Idea for you."

I look up warily.

"Why don't you spend a few hours a day volunteering at the hospital?"

Or not.

I'm not great with kids, and a job without pay? Why can't I just veg? Only I don't talk to Aunt Ellie the way I sometimes talk to my mom—or sometimes, don't talk to her at all.

I don't want to be thrown out, so I don't talk back, but I exhale, so she gets it. "What could I do there?" I ask, finally.

"Lots of things," she says brightly, getting on my nerves. "They need people to read to the kids, bring books to the patients, run errands. I'm sure they'd love to have you."

"Probably have to be eighteen. I'm not old enough."

"Yes, you are. They use volunteers your age all the time."

⁓⌾⁓

It's not something I can explain to Aunt Ellie, but the truth is, bed is at the top of the list of places I want to be right now. And if I do go out, I want to sit by myself at the water after everyone is gone—especially him. I refuse to come off like a pathetic groupie.

Aunt Ellie is usually cool about things, only she isn't now. She's drawn a line in the sand and she stares at me, waiting.

"I guess I could go."

"I'm driving by this afternoon, I'll drop you." It's all

settled in her head, but she must read the look on my face because she comes back and sits on the edge of the couch.

"Sirena, helping other people has a way of making *you* feel better. Believe it or not, it lets you forget about yourself and your own problems and see things in perspective. You're not the first girl whose parents are breaking up and you won't be the last. Life goes on, and you have to live your life. Nothing is inherently good or bad, it's how you let yourself see it and react to it. Really, it's in your hands."

Did I have a choice?

She starts to walk out of the living room and then glances back at me.

"I'm *going*."

How I see things and react to them is in *my* hands? How could I feel good about my life when I didn't have one? No summer plans, no parents, no friends around and no real place to live anymore. What did that leave me? A dog friend and a fantasy? I go upstairs, stub my toe on the foot of the bed, and start to sob. I stand in the shower so she can't hear me.

eleven

Aunt Ellie's outside in the car by the time I'm dressed. We drive through town to the hospital without more talk. The best I can hope for is a flat tire, but it doesn't happen.

The double doors at the front of the hospital spring open by themselves as if they're under some invisible power. To my left is a separate entrance with a red neon sign: *Emergency*.

Compared to the hospitals at home, this looks like a small clinic. Only three floors and few people in the lobby. At the information desk there's a woman in a pale pink jacket with a button: *Volunteer*. Next to her is a vase of flowers that looks like it was left behind by a patient who didn't want it.

"Who do I see about volunteering?"

Her small, sympathetic smile says she understands more about me than she possibly could. "Have a seat, dear."

I land on a hard, blue plastic bench opposite a girl my age engrossed in *People*. She sits with her skinny legs wound up like a pretzel. That reminds me of Marissa, who right now is kayaking, playing tennis, or rock climbing while I'm waiting to work for no pay. I want to call her and cry, only sleep-away camps pride themselves on not staying connected. No laptops, zero cell service in the mountains, and fewer pay phone privileges than prison inmates. That left writing letters, which arrive about as fast as they did in the 1800s.

But I look on the bright side.

No buggy bunks or thin, ancient mattresses for me this summer. No bug juice. No after-camp love handles from carb loading. No bleeding mosquito bites. No gross, bugafied bathrooms...

"Sirena?"

A woman in a green hospital jacket stands in front of me, smiling expectantly, and I crash land. At least I'm a celebrity, because the whole town already knows my name. I resist offering my autograph and smile weakly. "I was wondering if you needed a volunteer."

"We're a small hospital," she says, "but there are always patients who would welcome company, and if you'd like to read to the children or play games with them..."

"Should I come back tomorrow, then?"

"You can start today." She points to the elevator. "Go to Three and ask for Mary Carol, she's the social worker. She'll show you around and get you started."

I'm given a stack of papers to fill out, and in the time it takes to answer everything, I could have written a term paper. I give it all to Mary Carol and she starts to look it over when her phone rings. "I have to take this," she mouths. She points to a sign outside: *Patients' library and lounge.*

I follow the arrow down the corridor, past a nurse pushing a cart holding orange plastic bottles of pills and white pleated cups. Just before I get to the front desk, I stop short.

That's when I see his back.

My heart senses him before my brain does. Broad shoulders, a narrow waist. White letters: EMS on the back of a navy T-shirt. Low-slung jeans.

What is he doing here?

He's talking to one of the doctors, and I watch as he lifts a hand to the back of his neck. He's considering something—I can read his body language now. He shifts from one foot to the other, his slow dance of impatience.

I slip back into the hallway out of view like I'm in the frame of a movie spinning in reverse. I don't want look like I'm lurking so I duck down and tighten my shoelace. Casually, I glance around the corner and watch him heading down the corridor. A young nurse turns to him and smiles. He stops to talk. Jealousy stabs me.

When he turns away, I jump up and follow his long-distance shadow. I step out of his line of vision in case he turns as he waits for the elevator. I'm good at this—he doesn't know I'm there. Once he's inside and the doors close, I slip through the exit door, skipping down the three flights of stairs. My heart is punching at my chest. Will he be gone? Does it matter? What the hell am I doing? All I know is, I can't help it.

He's going through the outside doors as I reach the lobby. I follow him out and duck behind a post. He climbs onto a black motorcycle and revs up the engine, reaching into his back pocket for sunglasses and then the helmet behind him on the seat. The idea of sitting behind him on his Harley with my arms around him completely blows me away. He glances behind, starts to back up, but then stops when a girl calls out:

"PILOT."

She's about my age, or a little older. Blond. Denim cut-offs. A white tank top. A tan so perfect she might have been dipped. She makes a megaphone with her hands: "Wait up."

He turns toward her and I reach for my cell.

Click. I have his picture. *Have I stolen your soul?* My hand tightens around the phone.

I stand back hiding as he waves to her. She runs to him, her ash-blond ponytail swishing back and forth over her narrow hips. She kisses his cheek and hops on the back of his bike, closing her arms around his waist. She's at ease wrapping herself around him like a snake. They exchange a few words before he revs up the engine and they ride off together. I lurk in the shadow of the doorway longer than I have to. A scared little kitten, afraid to come into view.

twelve

"How was the hospital?"

I look up abruptly from *Teen Vogue*. "Oh...okay."

"What did you do?"

"They showed me the pediatrics floor and I went to the library and picked out books to read."

Aunt Ellie waits, expecting more. She gives up. "So when do you go back?"

"Tomorrow, I guess, in the morning."

"I have an appointment, otherwise I'd drop you, but you can take one of the bikes in the garage. It's a quick ride."

I like the idea of getting around by myself. I nod and go back to the models in fall clothes. The übercool with überlooks. Hundreds of dollars per hour just to show their faces. No decisions to make. They were set for life.

And me? One more year of high school, then college,

and I'm not sure how far away to go. I can't help thinking now of camp visiting day when my parents came up—together. What would happen now? Would it feel awkward and depressing for them to visit me at college together when they weren't a couple anymore?

I read a book about a girl with divorced parents who grew up in the fifties. It said she came from "a broken home."

Now that's me.

Broken home, broken life, broken spirit. Like a Looney Tunes Ophelia, my head starts to sing,

Humpty Dumpty fell off a wall.
Humpty Dumpty had a great fall.
All the king's horses and all the king's men
couldn't put Sirena together again.

Aunt Ellie glances over at me. I pretend not to see. She shakes her head, finishes drying the dishes, wipes her hands on the towel and goes into her office. I go upstairs carrying milk and two doughnuts, the unhappy girl's default snack. I take out my hot pink stationery box so I can write to Marissa. I bought it two years ago just before camp. I remember standing in Target trying to decide which I liked better, the paper with the red hearts or the one with the borders of curly pink ribbons, as if things like that truly mattered in the world.

Now for the first time in six years, only Marissa is away

for the summer. "I'm in a totally great bunk," she said in her first letter. "And guess what? I already have a part in the camp play."

YES, whoopee!

She's obviously fine without me. She's a CIT and it's her last year unless she goes back as a counselor. We thought we'd be together, that we'd end our six-year tradition at the banquet at the end of August with plastic wine glasses of "champagne." I had a fake ID and we even talked about sneaking into town for a six-pack—something real to toast with.

I make a lame effort to sound enthusiastic:

Hey BF, camp sounds so cool—and wow, the freaky mayor's wife part in Bye Bye Birdie!!—OMG, congrats!

Things here are close to comatose. Let's see. No socials, but there's a fairly hot—no, strike that—incendiary lifeguard at the town beach. Only don't get excited, he's already taken, and anyway, even if he wasn't, he's so high on himself and uninterested in me—long story; I'll save it. Otherwise...I started volunteering at the local hospital.

I put the pen down. Should I tell her about today? As soon as I start writing, everything I wanted to forget pours out.

I was in the hospital—my first day, Marissa—and, while I was there, just on my way downstairs to get a soda, a man holding a small boy in his arms rushed through the doors. His clothes were soaked with blood—it looked like he was shot. Then I saw the boy's head. He couldn't have been more than six or seven. Blond curls hung off the side of his face—encrusted with blood. I felt like I couldn't breathe when I saw him.

Between deep breaths the father, who was so upset he could barely get the words out, explained that his son, Cody, was riding his mountain bike without a helmet. When he tried to race a friend he lost control, fell off his bike, and was thrown down a hill. He landed hard on some rocks. His parents were wild when they brought him in. His father kept repeating, "It was his birthday present, it was his birthday present," as if how could fate be so cruel as to turn on an innocent kid enjoying his birthday present? As if everything else in the world made sense, except that.

The head wound was so terrible, and he was unconscious. The doctors weren't sure how bad it was. They had to do tests, they said. They rushed the boy onto a gurney and wheeled him into the emergency room. I don't know what happened after that. I just stood there frozen. Later on I was riding up in the elevator with two doctors. One leaned over to the other. "How's the kid doing?" he said. The other doctor just shrugged. "We don't know yet."

I freaked, Marissa. Only, I don't know why. Was it that it was a little kid in critical condition? Blood everywhere? His parents' faces? Or the kid being wheeled off to a room where they pulled the curtains closed fast, as if from then on, everything was so bad that they had to hide it from you?

There are so many things in the world that scare me. Are you like that too? I feel like such a baby. I'm almost seventeen and I should be able to handle things like this. Sometimes I feel like I'm falling apart. I'm all alone here without my parents and you, and the people you love are the glue that keep you together.

Sorry to be such a downer telling you all this—especially when everything for you is so perfect—but if I can't tell you... You know? My aunt wants me to volunteer for the summer, but if this is what I'm going to be seeing, I don't know if I can handle it.

A little voice in my head tells me to toughen up, only I haven't figured out how to do that.

Other than needing head work...The beach here is the most perfect place to spend the summer. I'm going to start going on long swims like my aunt. I want to get into better shape so I can try out for the swim team in the fall. In the meantime, write and tell me more about camp. I want some of the normalcy in your life to rub off on me and get me through the next two months, so send good karma!

Love you and miss you terribly,
Sirena

I put a stamp on the envelope and sit with it in my hand. I think about Cody's accident and I'm crazed by the realization that in just a few seconds, everything about your whole life can change because you did something stupid. Cody was this happy, normal kid one minute, and then, because of a split second of bad luck when his parents weren't watching, everything changed and might never go back.

I get up finally and mail the letter. Aunt Ellie's garage is crowded with tools, picture frames, odd planks of wood, garbage cans, a dead washing machine, and old bikes. I find a mountain bike that's in better shape than the others and I take it out for a ride. After I'm nearly down the street, it hits me—*I can't believe I did that*—I'm not wearing a helmet. I go back and grab one.

I ride on the bike path along the beach. The color of the blue-gray ocean changes from every angle, at every hour of the day. It would be almost impossible to capture it on a canvas. I wish I had my camera. It would help to work from pictures so the light couldn't trick me. The sky looks like rain now and the water is as silvery as an icy pond in winter. I stop and lean the bike under a tree, taking off my helmet and wiping my forehead with my hand. I take a long drink of water and sit down. My shirt sticks to me.

I look over at the beach and see the painter Aunt Ellie told me about. That has to be him. He's sitting in front of an easel with a palette next to him. A big umbrella in a dark green-and-orange African print shades him from the sun.

A black dog, big as a bear, with a thick, glistening coat naps contentedly next to him.

I wish I had my sketchbook.

He's wearing a loose Hawaiian shirt in yellow and orange, There's no missing him. He's this...presence.

His skin is very brown, as if he spent all of his life in the sun. He seems to sense I'm there because he turns his head and smiles. I smile back. Why don't I feel embarrassed? I leave my bike and cross over to him. "Antonio?"

He nods.

"I'm Sirena, Aunt...uh, you probably know...Ellie's niece."

"You're an artist, too."

"Well, I..."

"Sit down." He gestures to the dog. "Meet Edna," he says, leaning down to pat her head. He reaches into a brown paper bag and takes out a box of chocolate chip cookies. Edna opens her eyes, as if on cue. "Not for you, Edna," he says. "They can't eat chocolate," he says. "Sad, eh?" He holds the bag out to me.

I nod and take a cookie. The chips are slightly melted. I smile at him.

"Mmmm."

Antonio looks the way I imagined him. Thick, dark hair mixed with gray and eyes the color of cocoa. He's not sad like some older people, with a lost look in their eyes.

He's vibrant and so handsome that he looks like an actor. There's a contradiction about him, though. His eyes look like they've seen and lived everything, but his private face seems used to keeping a world of things inside.

I can't help being drawn to him like a wise teacher. I sit with him for a while just watching him paint, feeling no need to talk or fill the silence. His brush looks old, like an antique. The handle is ivory and it's delicately carved. He takes a long time between brush strokes, as if each one represents a separate decision.

"You've been a painter for a long time."

"Since I was a little boy—six years old."

He says it like it was an eternity ago. "Did you teach yourself?"

He nods. "And you?"

"I can't remember not drawing. But I started taking art classes after school, during fifth grade."

"It's wonderful, no, to draw, to paint?

"Yes...but...it's not always easy, at least for me. Sometimes everything just comes out awful, like total garbage." I sink my toes into the sand. "It's so hard, you know?"

Antonio keeps painting. Did he pay attention to what I said?

"The struggle," he says, finally. "That's so big a part of it. You work, you work harder. It takes everything inside of you...all your energy...your soul." He makes a fist and pushes it in toward his stomach. "You have to struggle to make art. It consumes you. But art chooses *us*, and in the end, the pain is worth it, no? There are the small... glorious...triumphant moments." He holds up a fist.

His face softens as though he's remembering something personal and special to him. Then he looks in my eyes.

"To make art is to be *alive*, Sirena." He narrows his eyes. "It's like to love."

I pick up a pink shell in the sand and study its smooth, fluted surface, closing my hand around it. "Well, I'm not... there yet."

"But you will be, one day," he whispers. "I promise you. Your whole life...it is *ahead* of you, Sirena." He reaches out and for the briefest moment, closes his large hand around mine. Then he releases it and turns back to his canvas.

⁓⊙⊙⁓

I sink back in the sand and study his hands as he works. Short, square nails. One is half black, as if it had been hit. The back of his hands have brown shadowy spots on them. Veins bulge out like worms beneath the skin. They're strong hands that could lift the earth. Every part of him looks strong, from his thick neck to the powerful forearms. He

73

used to be a fisherman, Aunt Ellie said. At one point he looks over his shoulder at me and smiles.

"I guess I should probably be going. You're trying to work."

"Stay, please," he insists. "I don't often have such fresh air around me—Such fresh, beautiful air." He laughs.

"My aunt's expecting me, but I'll come back and see you again." I scratch Edna's head and she rolls onto her back so I can scratch her stomach.

"Bring your sketchbook, so you can work next to me."

"Maybe it'll help."

"We'll help each other," he says.

I get up and turn to go when Antonio looks up peers into my eyes. "Don't be sad, *querida*," he says, softly.

I look at him curiously. How did he know? But by then he's looking ahead of him.

"This," he says, almost to himself looking at the slant of the sun. "This is the time I was waiting for."

I ride my bike along the beach feeling calmer than I have in a long time. Did something from Antonio's serenity transfer to me? Was something like that possible? Or was I just happy to have made a friend, even if he was the oldest one I had ever had. I laugh to myself.

Dear Marissa: well, I met a really cool guy today. Only don't get excited—he's eighty!

When I get into the house, Aunt Ellie is cutting up a salad.

"I met Antonio."

"I figured you would. Did you find him on the beach?"

I nod.

"And you immediately fell for him, right?"

I look at her and grin. "How did you know?"

"It's unbelievable," she says. "The man has that effect on everybody."

thirteen

By the end of the week they've moved Cody upstairs to a private room. I poke my head in. Is he up? His eyes look open, but when I get closer to the bed I see that he's fast asleep, his pale brown hair now silky clean.

He sleeps peacefully one moment, then suddenly his eyes dart up, then down. What kind of thoughts are in his head? Does he know what happened to him? Can he remember? Will it scare him and make him afraid to get back on his bike?

Just after I learned to ride a two-wheeler, I fell off and fractured my ankle. For years after I'd wake up during the night with a start as my mind replayed the fall. It took me a long time to get on my bike again.

On the side of Cody's face that hit the ground there's a bandage, but it doesn't totally cover the beginning of a red scab. The area around it is green, yellow, and purple and it's swollen. The skin looks like plastic wrap pulled over the top of a bowl. An IV is attached to his arm and he's on a heart monitor. I watch the hypnotic pattern of the green zigzag line as it goes up and down, over and over, turning the heartbeat into modern art. Is it a normal scribble? When he was first brought in, he was on a ventilator, a machine that breathed for him. Now he's off it. That has to mean he's better.

I read a poem to him, even though he's sleeping, whispering the words. Can fields of yellow daffodils erase memories of blood and pain? Can he hear me? Will he turn toward me, the way a plant leans toward the sun for warmth, light, and survival? I want to know we've connected, but I search his face and swallow, involuntarily.

I shut the book and squeeze his marshmallow hand. He doesn't respond. He's a limp rag doll who I want to take home to keep on my bed, like a new stuffed animal. "Bye, I'll visit you tomorrow," I whisper.

I start to leave, then stop, guilty about walking out on him. I'm sure his parents are nearby, but right now he's so alone. I'm not supposed to fall apart. I'm there to help kids, but now I'm the helpless baby trying to muffle my sobs.

Sirena, you're such a mess.

Mary Carol must have heard me because there she is at the door. "Are you all right, Sirena?"

"I don't know what it is that gets to me...He's not *my* child, I don't have a little brother or even know any kids like him."

"We all struggle with how to deal with kids who are sick or hurt. It's hard for all of us. It makes us realize how helpless we are to prevent it."

"But a kid...nearly getting the life smacked out of him..."

Kids have to be protected and spared, and if they're not, it's unfair, and their parents have failed them.

I can't stop crying. "I better go."

She shakes her head. "Things around here get to all of us. It never gets easier, but eventually...you handle it."

⁓⊱❦⊰⁓

I walk along the corridor and spot his parents sitting together on a bench, eyes hollowed; mouths pinched as if someone has stolen their insides. Outside the building, out of view, I crouch down, dropping my head to the ground. It feels like I'm going to be sick.

fourteen

I'm glad Aunt Ellie isn't home. I want to sleep, not talk to anyone. What I feel is too complicated for words. I get into bed, only I dream about bicycles and accidents. I fall and I'm trapped under something, something heavy, and I can't get away. My body jerks and I wake up.

To get my mind off Cody, I take out my sketchbook and sit on the window seat. I flip open my phone and there he is, straddling the Harley, his face serene and composed, his yellow, sun-streaked hair blown back off his face.

Pilot.

I wouldn't say his name outside, out loud, but here in my room with no one around...

Pilot. Pilot. Pilot.

I say it again and again to see what it sounds like to my ear, to try it on my tongue. Pilot. Pilot, as if the more

I say it, the more he becomes mine. It suits him, but why? I brainstorm with myself. Associations? Guide. Leader. Driver. Explorer. Initiator. Someone independent. It works. It's perfect for him. The alternatives are laugh-out-loud funny. Boring names. Common ones. George, Jack, Steve, Thomas, Allen, Jed, Fred, Martin, Mark. He wouldn't have any of those names. He couldn't.

He isn't *like* anyone else.

I work at transferring the face in front of me to paper, never mind that his eyes are hidden behind sunglasses, as if he doesn't want me to see or know his eyes and his soul. The shape of the head first, then the mouth, which is easier because his lips are full, almost bowed.

How would he kiss?

I put the pen down. How much of himself would he put into it? I dream of making out with him for hours, feeling him next to my skin and burying myself against his warmth, inhaling his sweetness like a drug I can't take enough of. I think about seeing his green eyes flood with longing and watching his face come alive as we kiss harder and harder. We'd spend the night on the beach inside a tent, zipped into a sleeping bag. My initiation. My innocence offered up to him and no one else.

La petite mort, the little death.

When we read about *la petite mort* in a book about literature, Marissa and I laughed so hard we were in pain.

It's the euphoria, or altered state, you're left with after reading something astounding, it said. Then we looked it up. We saw what it really meant: the spiritual release after orgasm.

"*Omigod.*" Marissa burst out laughing.

Now I sit staring out at the water, hugging my sketchbook to my chest, my eyes burning, my throat dry with longing, thinking of that now. Thoughts of him flood my mind, taking it over. I'm his robotic toy, remote controlled.

A car horn blast brings me back to reality.

Focus, I tell my head. I keep on drawing. The mirrored aviator sunglasses on the bridge of his nose. That impenetrable, unflinching coolness. His body armor.

The harder I try to sketch him, the worse it looks, as if hard work is at odds with inspiration and creativity. Everything is wrong. It looks nothing like him. It's awful, terrible, stupid, and embarrassing. I'm not an artist, I'm a kindergartner and a fraud. I have no talent, so why am I pretending?

You have to struggle to make art, Sirena.

But Antonio isn't sixteen, he's eighty. Will I have to struggle that long? Pinta, an oversized Calico, sidles up and sits next to me. She looks at the picture and yawns.

"You're being kind."

Trust your eyes, they tell you, only mine aren't seeing. It doesn't help that the picture in the camera is tiny and indistinct, worse than a fleeting image on a surveillance video. For some freaky reason I wonder if the problem isn't the matchbox-size cell phone picture, it's that some elusive quality of his can't be captured, which makes no sense, but maybe it comes with living in a house with ghosts and suspecting that everyone in the whole world may have a supernatural presence.

I rip the papers from my sketchbook and crumple them up. I try over and over. I can't get his face. I can't see it, I don't know it. How can I capture something I've never been close to for more than minutes? Even then I felt lost in a fever dream. The picture is useless. Did I really think it would help me to know his face? That's like trying to come up with the formula for the chemistry between two people attracted to each other.

I fold a sheet of paper into a plane and shoot it across the room. It crashes against the wall and slips to the floor. What I need is a close-up, otherwise I'll have to park myself in front of him, and how likely is that in this lifetime? I throw down my notebook. I want to punch something.

Flashback to months back. Me on the couch of a shrink. I went to her after they told me they were separating. My parents' brilliant idea, not mine.

She looked at me, a searching half smile on her face. "What are you feeling, Sirena?"

I was sitting on her brown suede couch, at arm's length from a box of Kleenex. The whipping tick of the gold alarm clock on her desk, the only sound in the room.

I leaned forward, about to explode. Go screw yourself, I wanted to shout, that's what I'm feeling. I felt like putting my fist through her door as I ran out of it. Why was it *her* business what I was feeling? And anyway, what possible good could come of *me* telling *her* what was inside my head? Could she change my life? Was talking about it going to make everything suddenly better? I met her patient stare.

HATE ME, DON'T PITY ME, I wanted to scream. I showed up for one last futile session.

I get on my bike and ride to town. I haven't been to Antonio's gallery yet, and I want to see his work up close and study what he does—even use him as my model. I smile at the thought of him in his red canvas director's chair surrounded by his quirky props, most of all Edna, benignly watching and waiting, wise to the world around her.

⁓◦❦◦⁓

Not hard to find the gallery. Only one store in town sells paintings and crafts. The door is open, but I don't see anyone.

"Hello? Hello?"

A glass counter in the front holds earrings, pins, woven bags, and wall hangings. I walk past it.

In a large city, someone greets you, even takes you around. But here when shopkeepers leave for lunch or coffee, they don't bother locking up. You can roam free and if you need help, you just try back later.

I wander around the gallery. Most of the paintings are seascapes that look like they were done by beginners. It wouldn't surprise me to find numbers beneath the patches of color.

I turn and see a doorway down a small corridor to my left. The office? But it's not, it's a separate gallery room. On the opposite wall, there's a painting that's different from all the others.

It's Antonio's, I can feel it.

It's dreamlike and romantic, a pastel of hazy clouds in a blush pink and tangerine sky, veined with faint streaks of turquoise. I want to be lying on the beach under that sky, or at least seeing the painting first thing in the morning.

Art changes the way you see the world, my art history teacher said, and Antonio's magical picture opens my eyes to the sky as a changing canvas and nature as the world's most brilliant artist.

There's another picture. Edna. She sits tall at the edge of the ocean, her coat black as brilliant as if she was brushed right before she was painted. She's supremely content, as if she's thinking there's nothing she'd rather do than sit for Antonio, as long as it takes.

I turn and see another of his paintings. It's haunting and complex. I can't stop staring. It's only paint on a canvas, I have to remind myself, because it seems to reflect a living, breathing soul, pulsing with life and energy.

Pilot.

I'm not surprised Antonio would paint him. He has an eye for beauty and any artist would be drawn to that face. Antonio had no trouble with the shape of the head or the perfect proportions of his face. I want to reach into the canvas. I lean so close my lips are nearly touching his. I expect to feel the heat of his skin and inhale his sweet, addictive scent. The picture sends bolts of energy inside me.

What in the world is going on with me?

I turn abruptly, my heart pounding, and look behind me, embarrassed. I'm relieved that no one saw.

I turn back to the picture and bathe in its beauty. Most of all, Antonio captured Pilot's eyes, their hypnotic quality and his disarming, open-eyed stare. Guarded, yet vulnerable, as if he looked up and was caught in a private moment. The magic is that this is a painting, not a photograph, because it offers the split second of truth that comes through the eye blink of the camera.

I can't afford the painting, but I hate the idea of someone else owning him and taking it away so I'll never be able to see it again. I don't want anyone else to have it. I don't want anyone else to have him. I start to leave and head for the door, turning back for a last look, now from a distance. His ocean-green eyes hold mine, following me wherever I go. His spirit lives in the canvas. I expect it to speak with the soft, seductive sound of his voice.

I glance around quickly. There's no one else in the gallery. Is there a security camera somewhere? Are people watching? If they are, the camera's well hidden. This doesn't look like a high-tech gallery, though—not at all the kind of place that would spend money to hide a camera. Am I just trying to reassure myself? Once the thought of what I want to do enters my head, it doesn't let go of me. I'm a little kid again ready to have a tantrum.

I want it.

Sirena, you can't, my head insists. Don't do it, don't do it. Don't be stupid. "Get over it," as Marissa would say. "Don't be dumb and throw your life away." Miss Goody Two-Shoes, my friend Aaron used to call Marissa. He loved to bait her, but she didn't care.

"You have to live with yourself," she always said, following her head, not her heart. Maybe that's why we got along so well, we balanced each other out.

Only now I ignore the clashing voices and reach out, carefully lifting the painting off the wall. I slide it inside my canvas shoulder bag. It fits perfectly, as though it belongs there inside with me. That gives me justification and comfort. I glance at the empty nail on the wall, the white space.

Sorry, I feel like scrawling. Instead, I slip out of the gallery as quickly as I came in, sneaking glances behind me and walking down the street slowly and casually. Everything is the way it should be.

"Sirena," someone calls out. I stop short and turn, my heart thumping erratically. Who is that girl? I don't recognize her. She's waving, but then I realize it's to someone farther down the street, not me. She calls out again, only this time I realize that the name she's calling is "Rita."

I head to the spot where I left my bike and put on the helmet. I take deep breaths and look around casually. Is anyone giving me strange looks?

Calm down, Sirena, You're fine.

But my heart doesn't buy it. It's still slamming. I hop on my bike and head to Aunt Ellie's. As I'm pedaling home, I slow down momentarily as a loud siren closes in on me. Someone saw you, someone saw you, a voice in my head shrieks, keeping pace with my staccato heartbeat. I start pedaling faster and harder, refusing to turn around. The siren gets louder and louder. In my side view mirror, I see a row of flashing red lights on top of the police car behind me and I hold my breath.

fifteen

*H*ow could you do that, Sirena? Are you crazy?

Whatever you do, don't tell your aunt, don't tell anyone, or you'll get in huge trouble. Anyway though, I love the drawing you did of the painting. Do you know how much talent you have? I am so envious. I can barely write my name, I swear. I don't know how you do it. Pilot is sooo hot. I showed everybody in the bunk. They think he looks like a movie star or a Calvin Klein model. Those sleepy, sexy eyes! Does he know you drew his picture? Does he have any idea?

Listen, just a thought. Sneak back into the gallery again at lunchtime and return the picture. Take a picture of it first and then just give it back. Seriously, think about it. I don't want my BFF to go to jail!! Do you know how totally horrible those prisons are for kids? There's one in Louisiana that makes kids eat rancid food and doesn't have air-conditioning and it's over *a hundred twenty degrees in summer! Kids have died there! Anyway, if you get busted, that will totally kill college, you know—you have to put that on the application!*

Nothing riveting on this end. Great bunk, except for one total geek who I'm sure will go to Harvard because she's got a 2,000 IQ. And get this, she reads Silas Marner for fun and brought a set of the classics with her. I swear! We had our second co-ed baseball game and I got two runs, which I think impressed the hell out of a kind of snooty Brit named Geoff (Jeff in plain English) Whelan who's kind of cute except for bad teeth. I will keep you posted. Report to me immediately on any more sightings or run-ins with BG (blond god).

(P.S. I swear I've gained fifteen pounds. I look like a total blimp. I hate the carbs here!)

Love you and miss you more than you can imagine!
Marissa

I was proud of the picture and I hesitated before I sent it. But I needed to show it to Marissa, if only to confirm that it wasn't only me who saw something so ethereally beautiful and rarified in his face.

Then there was the painting.

I had never done anything like that before. If my parents found out they'd blame themselves, the divorce, the stress on me of being sent away from home. But it was none of that. It was simply a case of want, need, and no choice.

I had to have it. It was as close as I'd ever get to him.

Would I eventually be found out? Would the cops come knocking on my door and cart me off in handcuffs? So far, I'd been lucky. None of the police cars were chasing me. Every time I hear a siren, though, my heart jumps. I wait at the window until it passes before leaving the house, even though that's totally stupid. I mean, if they knew it was me, wouldn't they just come and get me? Why would they wait, to see if I took more stuff?

What's strange is that there's been nothing in the local paper. There isn't much crime here, but when there is, the paper writes about it—drunk driving, speeding, or the theft of a lawn mower or bike. Since it was a painting in a gallery, maybe it wasn't considered a huge deal. Either that, or the gallery owner didn't realize it was gone, or didn't care. It wasn't a Picasso, but still...I was a thief.

~✦~

I swim for part of the afternoon and it's a welcome distraction. I can go farther now without getting winded. After I get back to the blanket, I dry off, then bike home along the beach. I slow down suddenly, confused. Antonio. Guilt washes over me. Why is he not in his regular spot?

Then I see.

"Sirena," he calls. "Come work with me. We have a model."

My stomach tightens.

Pilot. It couldn't be more embarrassing if he were nude. I hesitate.

"Sirena," he waves me over, impatiently. Sweat eats into my suntanned skin. I work at acting relaxed. "I don't have my sketchbook, Antonio."

Pilot turns to me, taking me in.

"I have another," Antonio says. "Come, he's such a good model."

I take the pad and pencil from Antonio. "You know each other, yes?" he says to both of us.

A hum of acknowledgement escapes my lips.

"How are you?" Pilot says, softly, his voice as calm and lyrical as music. I swear, his eyes are laughing.

I work at taking a breath and slide into the sand close to Antonio. "Good," I murmur.

The space cadet begins to sketch.

He's a kick-ass model. Perfect repose. There's not a nervous bone in his body, he holds that still. I get down as much as I can, reasonably happy with the outline of his head, the angle of his jaw, the strong curve of his shoulders and the banded muscles of his arms. It must be the nearness of Antonio that helps, if that's possible. He looks down at my picture after a few minutes, studying it.

"Maybe the face now?" Antonio says. We both start a new page.

Pilot shifts from leaning back on his elbows to sitting up, legs stretched out in front of him, leaning back on his hands. He tilts his head back, his eyes focused on me, without blinking.

Whose character study is this?

My eyes meet his, then flit back to the paper, my safety zone, a respite from the tension between what's real and physical, which for me seems to smoke like a live current.

"Ten minutes," Pilot says, suddenly dousing the flame. He has to go back to work, this is his lunch hour, I realize. My heart sinks. No, I want to insist. How can I stop? My hand works faster, racing the clock.

He glances down to check his watch, and finally stands to go, squeezing his eyes, shaking his head as if he's waking from a trance. He reaches overhead to stretch and I look away.

Antonio puts his hands together as if in prayer. "My dear Pilot, thank you." I murmur in agreement. As he walks away, his eyes glance down at my sketch. *What does he think?*

He saunters off without giving me as much as a hint. Antonio puts his pencil down and turns to look at me. Involuntarily, I yawn.

"Sleepy, Sirena?"

I nod.

"All the concentration, it can be tiring, no?" He smiles as if he understands more than he says.

sixteen

I bike to the hospital to see how Cody is doing, even though I'm off for the weekend. I stop at the library to pick out books for him and then make my way along the corridor to his room.

The walls of the children's wing are decorated with crayon drawings done by the kids. I love the spontaneous way they express themselves and the exuberance in their work. The pictures of happy kids are oversized, filling the paper with images of themselves and their families with zany ear-to-ear smiles. In one, the sun is the size of a basketball with straight lines like spokes of a wheel jutting out in all directions. The colors are bright and bold, the strokes free and open.

Then there are the sad kids, the troubled ones. Their figures are small and cryptic. There's darkness in their short, hard lines, as if their creativity is locked inside a prison of pain.

I get to Cody's room and think I'm in the wrong place. The balloons at the foot of the bed are gone. So is the stuffed animal menagerie that surrounded his TV. The bed is stripped, the mattress bare. Everything is lifeless and sterile. I check the number next to the door.

It's not the wrong room.

It's like he never existed.

I run to the nurse's desk. "Jane, where's Cody? What happened?"

She looks at me sympathetically. "Back in the ICU, Sirena," she says in almost in a whisper. "There were complications."

"Like what?

"He started having seizures and vomiting."

I'm not a doctor, I don't understand this, but her face tells me all I have to know. "What's going to happen to him?"

She shakes her head. "We just don't know. It's hard to tell at this point."

"He's just a little boy."

She reaches out and touches my hand. "I know, honey. It's never easy working here, especially in Pediatrics."

I walk back into his room and sit in the chair near the empty bed, my arms crossed over my chest, my eyes closed.

Finally I get up and walk to the window. Birds are circling in a big grassy field as if they smell food and are ready to swoop down. I think of the pterodactyls. One creature surviving at the expense of another. The coldness of nature. Where does a little child fit in? Whom would he fall prey to?

Just outside the door I see Pilot. *Why is he here?* He steps into the room and looks around.

"Where's Cody?"

He's been caught off guard, setting off a rush of nervousness and uncertainty in me.

"I...He's back in the ICU, I heard."

His eyes are shadowed with concern. "Since when?"

"This morning...He started having seizures."

I expect to hear him say something reassuring to give me hope; instead he disappears into the hallway.

⚬⚬⚬

On my way out I pass the chapel. I've never been inside it. I can't remember the last time I was in church. Now I should be first in line at confession.

You're a thief, Sirena.

Is this my punishment?

I tug open one of the heavy wooden doors. No white sterile rooms and life-support machines here. The room is bathed in warm, golden light. Candles flicker on the altar. Diffused light pours through a stained glass window. I feel

95

like I'm inside a Flemish painting.

I slide onto a cool wooden bench, lean back, and close my eyes. This has more to do with serenity than religion. I think of sanctuary and the power of distant prayer.

Is there anything I can do to help him? Some people are convinced that praying for others can heal them, even if you don't know them personally. Others swear it makes no difference. What would Aunt Ellie say? Science, science fiction, or something in between?

What I do know is that science and proof are apart from believing and, hoping so, I focus on Cody's skin and hair, his angelic face, his innocence, and all the life ahead of him. I have to do this, I have to help. I can't just stand there helpless and watch a baby die without trying, no matter how pathetic my help is. I squeeze my eyes shut, summoning up all the power in me to will him to get better. The alternative is unthinkable.

Tears pool in my eyes. Only now it's not just about Cody making it, it's about how everything will turn out in my life too, even though I know that's selfish. I want to draw on all the power in the universe to make him better so that he can go home. I want to make my parents love me too and I want to have a real home to go back to and a real life again.

I want to fix everything at once.

I ask for help as hard as I can as if there's a giant healing machine you can call on to steamroll over all your problems at once and make them disappear. I want to fix the road ahead and make it freshly paved without any bumps so everything in life will be smooth and easy and filled with joy. I don't care if that sounds like total make believe. It's what I want.

I curl up on the bench and sink into a cocoon of calm. I don't want to leave the protected world of the chapel. I close my eyes, and then the dreams come.

I'm on my bike pedaling furiously, trying to ride up into the sky like ET, fighting gravity, only I can't lift off and get away. The police are there, only they're wearing masks on their faces like doctors in surgery. Black curtains surround me, only they're not curtains, I realize; they're monks in dark robes holding crosses. They surround me. They're humming something in a strange language that sounds like the underwater music of the whale songs. It's so muffled I can't make it out. I can't understand anything because I'm underwater.

My eyes open. Day or night?

I get to my feet finally and walk to the door, unsteady. I squint in the harsh corridor lights that never shut off, whether it's day or night. The air smells of Lysol and old people and sickness. The magic doors spring open by themselves, as if a ghostly presence behind them is watching. I step outside, released into sunshine and warmth.

I bike home along the beach still numb from sleep,

studying the patchy clouds like Rorschach blots to explain the ever-changing mood of the sky. Then there's Antonio, and the same anxiety washes over me. The stolen picture. What do I do? He's wearing a black shirt instead of a colored one. An omen? I should have turned off and gone another way. I'm not ready to see him. I didn't prepare what to say or how to act. There are no distractions now. No model to hold our attention.

How can I smile and pretend everything's the same? I still haven't had a chance to tell him I saw his paintings and how much I loved them. I'm trapped. I start to pedal away, but he turns and calls out to me.

"Sirena."

The flitting butterfly caught in the net. Come up with something, anything, I tell myself. I get off my bike and slowly make my way to his chair, dropping down next to him in the sand. Edna looks up at me expectantly. Can she read faces?

Antonio is working on a new painting. It's darker, more stormy. I'm filled with wonder. How does he do it? Is it something I can learn?

"Your paintings are so alive. I wish I could paint like you."

He reaches out and touches my hand. "When it works, it's wonderful. When it doesn't..." He waves his hand out helplessly. "You know what Wordsworth said?"

I shake my head.

"'Fill your paper with the breathings of your heart.' Beautiful, no?"

I nod, my eyes tearing up. "Yes…"

I'm almost afraid to speak. Antonio glances at me and hesitates. He narrows his eyes, concerned. He turns back to his painting and we sit there for a few minutes without talking. He's using a new brush. Maybe that's for a painting with a different mood.

"Tell me," he says, finally.

I shrug, hugging my knees hard. He stops painting and turns to me, his eyes narrowed, questioning. I tell him about Cody. I need to talk.

"I'm scared for him, Antonio. I don't know what to do." I press my forehead on my knees.

"Children have energy, strong spirits, great resources," he says, slowly and deliberately. "Nature wants them to survive. By instinct, they fight. And there is…healing."

I look up, into his eyes. "Really?"

He nods and turns back to his painting, lightly touching the end of the brush to the canvas as if it's a test to see how faint he can make the color. For the first time I wonder if Antonio has a family and children of his own. Is his wife alive? What if she isn't? Would asking him make him sad? I don't want to pry. If he wanted to tell me, he would.

Instead I take deep breaths. I focus on his canvas.

"Have you sold a lot of paintings?"

He shrugs. "I sell some, I give some away. And you?"

I roll my eyes. "No one wants to buy any of *my* paintings. Not yet, anyway."

"I'll be your first client. When you're ready."

Now I can't think of anything *but* the painting of Pilot and I'm totally consumed with guilt. What if Antonio needed the money from a sale? What if he can't afford to buy food now? He's retired; maybe he doesn't have much money. I didn't think about anything like that, all I thought about was myself. I turn away slightly. It feels like something's stuck in the back of my throat and I can't swallow. I wish there was some way to fix what I did. He looks at me curiously for a moment and then turns back to his canvas.

"Antonio…" This may just end our friendship, but if I don't tell him, I'll never be able to spend time with him again without feeling guilty, and I know he'll figure it out and hate me more for not telling him.

He turns to me.

"I did something terrible and I wouldn't blame you if you never spoke to me again."

He knits his brows together questioningly.

"I went to see your paintings in town."

"Yes?"

"I'm really sorry about this, Antonio, I swear. I'll give it back."

"Give what back, Sirena?"

"The painting—of Pilot. I...I stole it off the wall."

"You stole the painting in the gallery?" His face darkens and he looks at me in disbelief, as though he's getting the facts straight in his mind. The change in his voice signals Edna, who looks up suddenly, as if she has to take everything in.

"Yes...I did."

He purses his lips. "So *you* are our little town thief."

"I am *so* so sorry, Antonio. I know it was wrong and I shouldn't have done it and I'll give it back, I swear."

He sits silently, as if in judgment, and then shakes his head up and down slightly as if some understanding has come to him. Just as quickly the darkness lifts and his face softens into an easy smile. He throws his head back and laughs, a deep, throaty laugh.

"What's so funny, Antonio? I stole your painting. That was awful of me."

"Why did you do it, Sirena? Tell me."

"I had to have it. I wanted to paint Pilot, too—it was before he modeled for us—only I'd never ask him on my own and, anyway, he wouldn't, I just know it. He doesn't even like me. "

He rubs the side of his face as if he's thinking and has come to some kind of wonderful decision. "No one has ever done anything like that. No one has ever stolen one of my paintings. It's wonderful, the passion. It makes me feel...exhilarated."

"What's so wonderful? I broke the law, Antonio. You could have me arrested."

"Yes, that's right. I suppose I could. But if you liked the painting so much you felt you had to have it, no matter the cost to you, then that's the biggest compliment to me and to my work, don't you see?"

"I'm not sure."

"You may keep it. I'll paint more pictures of him. That wasn't the first."

"I'd like to paint him, too," I blurt out, saying more than I should.

"He's handsome, no?"

I shrug.

"I'll ask him to sit for both of us again, for longer."

"No, please, Antonio, don't, don't ask him. Don't say anything. Really, it's okay." I jump up and get ready to get back on my bike. "Thank you for understanding. I felt awful about what I did. And please don't tell Aunt Ellie because she'll tell my parents. I was afraid the police would come to my house and arrest me."

Antonio smiles at me and shakes his head. I'm about to get on my bike and I stop and go back to him.

"Antonio, just one more thing. The theft was never reported in the paper. Did anyone realize it?"

"The gallery owner, he told me right away," Antonio says.

"So what did you do?"

"I told him I took it to fix it."

I hesitate. "But why?

"It was mysterious," he says, nodding. "And mysteries reveal themselves, Sirena. You just have to be patient... and then, eventually, the layers, they peel away, and the answers ...they come to you. Like healing."

seventeen

I wake up early the next morning and head to the mailbox. There's another letter from Marissa.

> You are so lucky not to be here. Three slutty girls snuck out of camp to go to a bar in town, but they got caught, so for the next week we're all paying the price. Lights out at nine, can you believe? Otherwise, it's unbearably hot and weirdo Geoff is playing games or something. Suddenly he's pretending that he doesn't want to hook up with anybody. I secretly think he likes this new girl in the next bunk. How totally sleazy is that?

I read the letter and was surprised to be happy not to be part of the group scene with the counselor police herding me from one activity to another. I don't have to answer to anyone here, except Aunt Ellie, and she's not a control freak.

I tuck the letter in my pocket and head outside. The air is cooler and there's a light breeze. It's a perfect day to bike. I pedal slower than usual on my way to the hospital. There are purple wildflowers growing along the road and I hop off my bike to pick some, binding the stems together with the rubber band from my hair. I lay them into my basket and keep going. On my way to Pediatrics I pass the chapel and stop. It can't hurt. Then I'll look for Cody. Whatever happens, I'll be strong and live with it. Maybe there is some higher plan, something we don't see or understand. It's all how you let yourself see things in life and react to them, Aunt Ellie says. It's about the words and feelings you attach to things that determine how you think about them and the effect they have on you. She's smart. She might be right.

After a few minutes in the chapel I go out into the brightness and walk the three flights of stairs. He won't be in the ICU anymore, I tell myself. He'll be back upstairs, completely better because I made it so—I put the idea out there to draw positive energy.

The scent of food is the first thing that reaches me when I open the corridor door. The dietitian is serving lunch. I scoot past a woman carrying a tray with a white plastic cover over a porcelain plate. Roast chicken. The other smell I pick up, like a dog detective, is mac and cheese—the all time favorite for kids.

I approach Cody's old room first. The door is closed.

I hesitate. Am I intruding? I knock softly and wait. No answer. Slowly I push it open.

My heart starts to slam.

There's no one at the nurses' station, so I run for the stairs. He's still in the ICU. Where else could he be? What was I thinking? I shouldn't be in the ICU—you have to be someone's relative to be let in—but I don't care. I run down the stairs and don't stop. When I go to the exit door and open it, the corridor is dark. Something's wrong. Where am I? I look up at the wall. B for basement. I'm too far down. God, is it the morgue? Out of breath, I go running back up to the first floor. My mouth feels dry and pasty; drums pound in my skull.

I approach the double doors and look through the glass windows. There are half a dozen beds, one next to the other in a semi-circle. I glance around the room. Some of the beds are hidden behind white cotton curtains. An old woman is getting a blood transfusion. I get a sick feeling as I stare at the plastic bag of maroon-colored liquid hanging next to her bed, a pillow of blood dangling from a steel IV pole. A rubber tube coated red runs into her arm. Other patients are sleeping, or unconscious. How can they tell?

I walk up to one of the nurses. She's writing in a patient's chart, the equivalent of the medical bibliography. She looks up at me finally. Why are you here? her eyes say.

"I'm looking for a little boy, he's about seven." I pause

to catch my breath. "Cody. His name is Cody O'Malley. He was here yesterday."

She shakes her head. We don't have children in here. Did you try the Pediatric ICU?"

"I...I didn't know there was a separate one."

She points outside. "First room on the left."

I feel stupid for not knowing. I walk down the corridor and see the sign above the door. The Pediatric ICU is smaller, only four beds. There are children in two of them. The other two are empty. I ask the nurse at the desk about Cody.

"I just started my shift," she says. "Let me check." She goes to her computer and types away, switching screens. It's a small hospital; why is it so complicated?

She looks up at me finally. "Transferred this morning."

"So he's better?"

"I guess."

I rush out the door and go back into the elevator, leaning back against the wall out of breath, almost faint. I lean over so blood runs to my head and I don't pass out. As the doors start to open I quickly stand up straight, taking deep breaths, trying to act normal. At the nurses' station I see a face I don't recognize.

"Cody O'Malley?"

"301."

seventeen

I hear voices in the distance as I walk down the corridor.

301. The door is open.

His parents sit on either side of his bed. For the first time they look up and make eye contact with me. His mother has color in her face. And the first thing I think? She's returned from the dead. My little rag dog has come back too. I see him truly alive for the first time, smiling and responsive.

"You're better," I blurt out.

"They gave me ice cream," he says, as though that's what made the difference. "And they said they'd bring more if I finished all they gave me."

"You're so lucky!"

"He is," his dad says, dropping his head. "We never expected..." His voice cracks and he turns abruptly staring hard out the window.

"We were all rooting for you," I say. It comes out too loud and euphoric, but no one seems to notice.

"They said I could go home soon," Cody says.

"We're supposed to go to Manhattan for a week's vacation," his mother says. "If he continues to get better, they'll discharge him and consider letting us go." She shakes her head. "He talks nonstop about climbing to the top of the Statue of Liberty."

"That's wonderful," I say, staring down at the flowers that I forgot I was holding. I reach out awkwardly and give them to her and she touches my hand lightly.

"I'll come back tomorrow with some games," I whisper to Cody, as I turn quickly to go.

I stop at the nurses' station outside and see Jane. "I can't believe it," I whisper. "He made a complete turnaround."

"We were all surprised," she says.

I think of what Antonio said.

"Children have energy, strong spirits, great resources. Nature wants them to survive. By instinct, they fight. And there is...healing."

I'm tempted to run to the beach to tell him.

Only I think he already knows.

⌁

Even though I'm not officially on duty, I read to some of the other kids, then go the pharmacy for an older woman who forgot to bring toothpaste and doesn't like the hospital brand. As I'm leaving at the end of the day, an ambulance pulls up.

"Car accident," a nurse tells the desk.

I rush to leave before they come in. I unlock my bike and pedal fast, taking the path along the beach.

eighteen

Visits with Antonio are part of my routine now. I stop to see him almost every day on the way home from the hospital. I've heard people talk about mentors, even though I've never really understood before what people like that are like. But now that I've met Antonio, I know.

His serenity and openness invite me to speak to him and sometimes I surprise myself and tell him more than I thought I would. The hospital, my home, my parents—even their divorce. He listens, but he never tells me what to do. Only sometimes he raises a hand to stop me. I wait for him to speak, but even then, it's just a few sentences, but with weight and spirit. He's almost…Godlike, and I'm in awe of him. I tell him about Cody and think about asking him whether he knew, but I look at him and his eyes answer.

Antonio knows all about me, but I don't know much about him, so I ask him about growing up in Brazil. I've never met anyone from there before. All I learned in school about the Amazon is that it's the world's largest river and that no bridges cross it.

He has a far away look in his eyes when he answers, as though his mind has traveled back home and he's telling the story from there, seeing it all again as if he's a child again.

"I was born in Manaus," he says. "My father was a shaman."

"A what?"

"A shaman is a healer of the rainforest who walks between the visible and the invisible worlds. Plants and spirits were his medicines." He shakes his head, as if in wonder. "He could look into other people's dreams," he says. "And he would have great dreams of his own, of vision and power."

"How did he learn everything?"

"He was an apprentice to another shaman. One passes the information to another. There are no schools for that."

"So when you were growing up and you got sick he'd find you the right plant and then pray?"

"Something like that," he says, holding a hand out in the air. "The rainforest is filled with life," he says, making a big arc with his hand. "There are a million different types of plants—almost three quarters of the animals and plants in the world. Everywhere you go, Sirena, there's wildlife and the music of nature and color, intense, brilliant color." He smiles. "They say there are four thousand different kinds of butterflies, Sirena. Can you imagine?"

Many Western medicines come from the rainforest, he says, but only one percent of all the plants have been studied for their use as medicines. "Some say the rainforest has a medicine for every disease."

"I want to go, I want to see it all."

"Ah, but there are more than plants and butterflies." He shakes a finger in warning. "Do you like mosquitos? There are clouds of them."

I shake my head. "I hate them, no."

"What about spiders, poison frogs, jaguars, tarantulas as big as my hand, and snakes—many, many snakes?"

I shake my head again.

"You know the anaconda?" His arm becomes an undulating snake.

"Only from a horror movie."

Antonio laughs. "Some say they have seen anacondas as long as sixty feet—a six-story building. Can you imagine?"

"Are you scared of them?"

"Only a fool wouldn't be."

Even though he never worked as a doctor, he studied with his father, he says, and learned how to heal himself with plants. "But cures come from spirits too. They enter your heart and soul. You have to give yourself over to the healing journey."

"But in this country, what do you do when you get sick?"

Antonio shakes his head. "I don't get sick," he says. "I've never been to the doctor."

"But if you did?"

"I'd boil the bush."

"What?"

"I'd take the plants I need."

"So you've never taken antibiotics for ear infections, or aspirin for headaches?"

"I don't get headaches, Sirena, but if I did, I would chew the leaves of feverfew."

"What's that?"

"Nature's aspirin—a plant that helps the pain. But to truly heal, you have to have a spiritual relationship with the plant. You have to want it to work. People in this country... they don't understand that. Medicine here can be cold, one sided. It treats the symptoms, not the disease. Here they don't understand that the mind and body are one."

He tells me about saving the Amazon jungle and the rainforest. "It's called the earth's lungs," he says, because it makes one-fifth of the world's oxygen.

But people rob the jungle, taking out the timber, he says. "Half the animals and plants in the world will be destroyed over the next few decades." Antonio puts down his paint brush. "People too," he says. "There used to be ten million Indians in the jungle. Do you know how many are left?"

I shake my head.

"One hundred, two hundred thousand, maybe."

"What happened to them all?"

"They were wiped out by Europeans who came to exploit the jungle and make money."

"Why can't anyone stop them?"

"The selfish move faster than the selfless," he says.

"Can't the government help?"

"They're part of the problem, Sirena."

When I finally remember that Aunt Ellie's waiting for me for dinner, the sky has turned velvet blue. I get to my feet. "I was so lost in what you told me that I'm late."

"Then you must go, you don't want to miss dinner."

As I start to pedal away, Antonio calls out to me. "Be careful, Sirena."

"Of what?" I get ready to shout back, but I stop. I'm too far away, and Antonio's a little hard of hearing.

nineteen

S o you like working at the hospital?" Mark says.

"It's fun to be with the kids," I say, surprising myself.

"You look happier." He glances at Aunt Ellie, who pretends not to notice.

While Mark is cooking, I look at the clock. "What time is dinner?"

"An hour or so."

"Can I go for a swim?"

"As long as the lifeguard is still on," Aunt Ellie says.

⁓⟨⟩⁓

He's not in his chair when I get there, but he's probably just somewhere else on the beach because he's still supposed to be on duty. I swim out past where the waves break. My arms are stronger now and I can go farther without getting winded. The sun is lower and the water feels cooler. I swim out past where the waves break, lying back and watching the light in the late afternoon sky. When I'm finally ready to turn and go back, I hear something in the water.

For no reason, I swim out farther and farther. I'm afraid to turn around, only I'm not sure why. My breathing gets faster, my head pounds. What is it? What could it be?

The sound gets closer and closer and then smack, my hand slams something hard. I look up, startled.

I turn and then I see what's come up next to me.

A fast-moving surfboard.

He's stretched out, naked from the waist up. He glides up alongside me, like a submarine that has silently risen to the surface.

I keep going.

"Time to get out," he says, finally.

"What?"

He turns the board abruptly, cutting in front of me. "Look how far out you are. You can't make it back on your own."

"How do *you* know?" Irritation creeps into my voice. I'm short of breath, but I work to hide it.

"Get on the board, Sirena. I don't want to have to pull you out." He pushes up to a sitting position, his legs straddling the board. There's room behind him now, only I don't know how to hoist myself up, or even if I can.

Before I can ask, he holds his hand out to me. "Here."

I grab his hand and he pulls me closer. I press down on the board with my hands raising myself high enough to swing a leg over and climb on. I breathe hard, trying to catch my breath. He shoots me a look of annoyance.

I *was* farther out than I thought. What if he hadn't been there? He leans forward and paddles with his hands as my eyes follow the fluid movements of his shoulder muscles under his smooth skin. We glide through the water without talking. Silence doesn't seem to bother him, but I feel the need to say something, anything, so he thinks I'm at ease and this is totally no big deal. Only small talk eludes me. My mind blanks.

His nearness alters my brain waves, the rhythm of my heart. My body downshifts from thinking to feeling...to longing.

I'm powerless, hard-wired to react only to him, like a helpless victim of my blood chemistry.

Can he tell?

He doesn't speak, but his presence does. His radar is everywhere, watching the beach in front of him, sensing me and everything around us. I draw energy from him as if it passes through his skin to mine, taking me to a more vivid dimension of feeling, being and knowing.

When we get close to where the waves break, he tilts his head back.

"Hold on."

He reaches back, his hand momentarily grazing my thigh. I lean into him, my arms tighten around his waist as the waves bounce us up and down, dousing my heat with their cool spray. We're skin-to-skin, two bodies melded together as one. I've forgotten about swimming out too far, or what I should have known. Everything is right now.

I don't want this to end.

I want to stay where I am with him, in the water, forever.

"I've never been on a board before," I whisper in his ear. "It's fun."

He glances back at me and a hint of a smile crosses his face. He stops paddling and we sit as the waves carry us up and shoot us down, again and again, each time propelling me against him.

We're connected now

And I'm in overdrive. Is this sane?

"I used to be afraid of the water." *Why did I tell him?*

"And now?"

"Not anymore."

"You should be."

I didn't expect that, not from him. "Are you?"

"It's more awe than fear. It's the power that draws me. But it's an unfair contest."

"Ocean worship? It sounds like a religion."

"Yes," he says with a smile. "The water is my god."

Then I want to enter your church.

But I don't say that.

⁓◦⊙◦⁓

We sit there together and time passes. Seconds? Minutes? I can't tell. I'm a giddy kid on a rocket ship ride, thrusting forward and back, up and down with the waves, until our precious time together runs out. How much longer do we have left, just the two of us, in our water world apart from the shore?

My lips nearly touch the back of his neck. His hair blows back, against my face, covering my eyes. I'm blind to everything but him. I cling to his waist inhaling his warm, coconut scent, my breath coming faster and harder than it should. Is this what making love feels like? How can he not sense my aching attraction, the sweet, intoxicating chemistry, the way the air is ignited between us?

I exhale against him in total surrender. He doesn't bruise, but does he shiver? Does he feel? Respond? I have to know, only what do I ask? As if in answer, he arches back against me, his cheek grazing mine.

"Sirena," he whispers.

120

twenty

At close to ten that night my dad calls. I'm on the window seat of my great ocean liner staring out at the crescent moon over the dark water. The ring startles me.

He sounds so alone. He's not used to being on his own or cooking himself dinner. I remember his microwave meals, frozen on the inside, the nights my mom had to go somewhere and he was in charge.

I also remember other things now, things that I tried to forget. The phone calls I heard, but weren't supposed to when I walked into his study without warning. The way his voice changed in a heartbeat, from low and intimate to cool and businesslike.

From wrong to right.

I block that from my head now.

He's staying at a friend's apartment for a while. He

went out for a hamburger and a beer or three, I'm guessing. He calls because it's his time to call. Okay, not fair, but they switch off. On even days my mom calls. Odd days, my dad. That way neither of them can blame the other for forgetting.

My dad isn't great on the phone. To him it's just a tool to give information or get it. He doesn't know how to fill up the conversation.

"So how's my girl?"

"Good."

"How's Ellie treating you?"

"Good."

There's an uncomfortable pause and I work to fill it.

"How's work?"

"Same old, same old."

My dad's a contractor and he spends six days a week fixing people's homes and, as he says, "making their dreams come true." That means remodeling big kitchens with islands and backyards with pools and spas. I think he's happier with a hammer, nails, and a glue gun than with people. He knows what to expect with tools. If they're treated the way they should be, there aren't too many surprises. Even if he had problems though, he wouldn't say. He'd think, what was the point? Pragmatic. That's the vocab word that suits him.

"So how do you fill your day?"

I tell him about practicing swimming and how I'm getting better at it, and about volunteering at the hospital.

Also about Antonio. "He's eighty years old and eighty years smart."

"So then I have nothing to worry about," he says, a smile in his voice.

If he only knew.

I wake closer to lunch than breakfast. The sweet, buttery scent of baking wafts through the air. More Norman Rockwell than my home-sweet-home, but whatever. On the kitchen stove there's a black iron cupcake tin filled with golden popovers with swelled heads like swollen muffin tops. Would Aunt Ellie have baked them even if I wasn't here? I decide she would. She does things like that. Baking bread and cakes, making homemade jam, even making pickles out of cucumbers which I didn't think you could do on your own. For her it's probably fun because she doesn't *have* to do it. No one comes home pissed off expecting dinner on the table.

"They're not hot anymore," Aunt Ellie says. She watches me stumble to the table. "You must have been tired."

I devour three popovers with strawberry jam and drink a glass of milk, studying the carton of organic low-fat milk. It's dark green and plum with little cows in a field like a Ben & Jerry's tableau. About as real as Legoland.

The kitchen is bright with sun. I notice for the first time that the green painted chairs around the table match the yellow-green grass outside. I also notice a slant to the floor. It's an old house, maybe that's why. Outside, the seagulls soar above the beach. They sound excited to be alive and have the entire sky to themselves, like ice skaters on an empty rink.

Everything is right about this new day. It feels like a new season, a fresh beginning. I look at the clock. He's been on duty for three hours. Is he thinking about me? Remembering? I can't get him out of my head. The feel of my arms around his waist. His warm skin against mine. His sweet smell. His nearness. I'm drunk with him and I don't want to get sober.

Even through my thick web of sleep, I saw his face. He was watching me. Dreams last only minutes, they say, but this lingered through the night, fading in and out as if we stayed together, entwined, stepping outside one universe and entering another where only we existed.

I wash my dishes, lost in thought. I find myself standing at the sink, staring at the bottle of green dishwashing liquid as if it's some odd find. I forget what I was planning to do next as if my mind and my body have separated inexplicably. Then I remember the shower. Slowly, I make my way upstairs.

Only now I don't use the white Dove soap in the

bathroom. I go to my makeup bag and get the soap Marissa gave me last Christmas. It was in a glittery sack with makeup from Sephora. On the pink wrapper, gold letters spell: *Intoxication*.

"For SPECIAL occasions only!" she wrote on the gift tag. She surrounded the note with red hearts from a glittery pen. I tear open the paper and sniff the sweet, musky perfume. When I come out of the bathroom, Will is sitting on my bed. He lifts his head and gets to his feet, ambling over to sniff my skin, detecting something new and curious, something he needs to take note of.

I put on shorts and a T-shirt and bike into town. Before I go the beach, I want to make a stop. The sun is warm on my face as I make my way along the main street. I steal a glance at myself in store windows—casual looks, so no one knows I'm checking myself out.

I look leaner now than when I first got here and my arms are stronger, even though they'll never be sculpted the way his are, each muscle so distinct he could pose for an anatomy chart, the kind they put up in the gym. My hair is full and the layers are longer and it's blonder from the sun. It cooperated today. It feathers around my face instead of poking out everywhere. I stand straight, not slumping, my mom's words echoing in my head: "Stand tall, head high, shoulders back."

I'm in the zone. I can handle shopping for a new

bikini; never mind that it'll blow my budget. I take a deep breath and enter Waterworks, a bathing suit universe with floor-to-ceiling racks as if bathing suits were the only things in the world anyone needed.

The girl behind the counter is busy with another customer. Good. I don't want help. The right suit will speak to me.

I find my size and push past the one-piece suits, the tankinis and bikinis in the all-black section. Too severe. No push-up bras either because you look desperate or like you just got implants. Hawaiian prints, but I'm not the flowery type.

Zebra? No, I'm not the jungle girl. Deep coral? There's a possibility with a solid blue top and a checked bottom, but I keep going. Whites, tans, crazy geometrics.

And then I see it.

A soft, celery-green bikini, perfect against tanned skin. Definitely glad my dad's not here because he'd cross his arms over his chest and veto it in a heartbeat. Low bottom, low top. Both pieces are outlined with tiny bands of ruffles. I take it off the rack and hold it against me in front of the full-length mirror.

I lock the dressing room door and drop my clothes on the floor. I slip it on, studying myself in the three-way mirror.

Perfect.

I take that as another good omen. Revealing, not slutty. I used to wish I wasn't five-foot nine. I was always taller than the boys in school. I don't wish that anymore.

~~~⚜~~~

I open the door and check myself out in the bigger mirror outside. The girl behind the counter passes me on her way to hang up an armful of suits in the dressing room next to mine and smiles. "Ohhh," she says. "You look hot."

I smile and shrug. What do you say to that?

As I'm waiting to pay, I see a necklace on the counter—a chunk of pale-green sea glass on a fine, gold chain. It's the same color as the suit. I slip it over my head and it falls just above the ruffled band of the top. The glass is pointed, like a shimmering arrowhead directing the eye to my cleavage.

I leave the store wearing the new suit and necklace with cut-offs over the bottom. I take my time, strolling to the beach, savoring the anticipation. It's hard to imagine that the reality could feel better than this. I almost laugh out loud, practically tasting my happiness. My heart flutters in my chest, the nervous kindergartener on the first day of school. Almost instinctively, I start to dial Marissa's cell number, and then stop. I'm insane. She's a million miles away with no cell service. What was I thinking?

I saunter along the sand, brushing past a family with a

cooler so large it could hold not only their entire dinner, but also a TV. I keep walking, passing teenage girls who look like they've OD'd on the sun because they're already third-degree fried. Finally I spread out the blanket and then, super casual; I turn my head in the direction of his chair, my north star.

Only now in a split second everything is different.

The world has fallen off its axis.

To the side of the lifeguard chair there's a blanket—with a girl on top of it.

The girl with the blond hair that reaches her butt—the maybe-aerobics instructor, the maybe-actress who jumped on the back of his Harley and locked her arms around his waist, holding him tight, just like I did. Jealousy spreads through me like poison and within seconds, I feel sick. I fight that, standing taller, resolute. I don't feel anything—my face works hard to show the world. I stare at her, trying to understand the enemy.

Snow-white bikini. I doubt it's a sign of her purity. Not too many girls can get away with a suit like that. If her nearness isn't enough, she's wearing his black cap that says *lifeguard*. He's kneeling next to her, smiling. She whispers something. Her jokes are obviously hilarious because now he's laughing. I've never seen him look so happy or relaxed.

I don't know this person. It isn't him. I discover he has teeth. I learn that he can smile. I think he's in love.

And I feel deathly ill.

Body blow.

Did I do something to deserve this?

If I had one wish right now, I'd wish that Marissa was here with me instead of being off at that stupid, God-forsaken baby camp at the other end of the earth, so she could hold me together so I don't totally self-destruct. She's the one person in the world who would understand this. She'd listen hard, then scrunch up her face and come up with a plan. Marissa doesn't wallow in self-pity. She takes action and thinks on her feet like a field commander.

"Life is short," she always says. Translation: Get up and get moving.

Only I can't make her parachute out of the sky right now and land next to me for hand-holding and strategizing, so I do the next best thing: I pretend real hard she is here, my crazy imaginary friend, and dream that while I stare out at the water and contemplate drowning, she'd be turning around and reporting back to me on what she's doing and what he's doing, sizing up how bad the whole mess looks. She wouldn't let me march off and go home, she'd grab me by the arm, make me sit down and lecture me.

"Sirena Shane," she'd say, "you're not going to roll over and play dead. Go walk past him and say hello and act totally cool. Stake your claim, even hang out with him and talk."

She'd tell me to ignore the blonde and act like I belong there.

"Just go pretend that everything is just the way it should be," she'd say.

The way it isn't.

Before I hit the ground running, I take out my mirrored compact and like a bad spy, I try to see behind me to get a fix on what's happening, which is humiliating and infantile and doesn't work anyway because the mirror is the size of an Oreo, and what I need is roughly the Hubble telescope. Only I can't help peeping. After a few seconds, the mirror catches the sunlight and the heat is about to burn a hole into my skin. It occurs to me to leave it there so I go up in flames, which is one way to deal.

Then I snap to, and do what Marissa would tell me to do:

Play the game.

I reach for ammo—the sparkly pink lip gloss in my bag that tastes like cherry, then some grapefruit cologne down the front of the suit. I push my sunglasses back on my head and tug the top of the suit down so it shows more. I stand tall, defiant.

This is totally no big deal. You can do this, my head insists.

My heart thumps erratically.

Code Blue.

If I were in the ICU now, they'd call for the crash cart and the priest.

Stop being a jerk, a little voice in my head says.

I walk in his direction because if this turns out to be the very last time all summer that I appear on the beach, I'm making dead sure he sees me in this bikini because I've blown my entire savings on it and it looks good, it does, it does, it does, it does. My head keeps replaying the voice of the salesgirl to buck up my crumbling ego:

You look hot, you look hot, you look...

I don't think I've ever looked better, at least that's what I tell myself now, or at least I thought it back in the store when I still had a functioning brain and a clear, working mind. I walk toward him and then slow down. It's a new day, everything's in a clearer—or maybe a blinding—new light. Have I been making this all up when it's crazy wrong? There's only one way to find out and the answer is about thirty, now twenty, now fifteen, now ten yards in front of me and looking more astonishing than I've ever seen him, his hair longer, wilder, more disheveled, all the better to set off the perfect planes of his angular face and his sleepy, deep-set, emerald eyes.

I get closer and closer, and as if he senses the vibrations of my footsteps in the sand, or picks up my scent on some primeval frequency, he turns slowly and stares hard in my direction. The easy smile grows fainter and fainter. His face turns more serious.

He's never looked this beautiful.

It almost hurts to look at him.

I'm interrupting though, I can tell. Getting in the way of whatever put the smile there before.

He not at ease anymore. Or happy.

What have I done?

He shifts from one foot to the other. I stop in front of him. For the first time I make out the slightest stubble of blond hair on his chin. His face first thing in the morning. He forgot to shave. Or didn't want to. Was he late for work? Why? My insides twist at the implications.

The air feels thinner. There's not enough of it, otherwise my lungs are failing. His eyes hold mine and I'm powerless. I feel arm-wrestled, pinned down, helpless. One hand goes up to the back of his neck, flexing his bicep to best advantage. There's a fine muscle pulsing in his jaw. I want to turn and run suddenly, but where? The girl at his feet on the blanket seems comatose. His cap shields her face from the sun.

"Hey," I breathe, so softly I'm not sure I said it or thought it.

And I wait.

"Sirena," he says, finally, nodding his head so slightly it's barely an acknowledgement. He licks his lips. He's uncomfortable, no hiding it. He doesn't want me around. I wait for a "How are you?" Even some pathetic attempt at a joke about whether I learned my lesson about swimming out too far.

But nothing.

Dead silence.

He looks away finally and reaches for his binoculars, behind him on the step of his chair. He steps back, at least I think he does, hiding his eyes from me and staring out at the expanse of beach, taking in everyone and everything.

Except me.

I DO NOT EXIST.

I've been snubbed.

Tasered.

Only I don't drop down which is unfortunate, because if I did, maybe then I'd get some shred of attention. Mouth to mouth resuscitation to get me breathing. He'd try to save me because it's his job, nothing more.

Or maybe he wouldn't bother. Been there, done that. Ignore her, she didn't learn her lesson.

Seconds go by, each one long, painful, agonizing. I can't let my face show what I feel. I can't. I can't, I can't. I try to look blank, emotionless. Cool. Does he see through it?

The sun, meanwhile, is so intensely hot that I'm about to faint, my mouth dry, my legs about to buckle under me. I have to get away from him, I have to.

I wait just an extra second.

After he's scoured the beach and made sure that no one is drowning will he finally turn back to me and say *something—anything* to acknowledge that I exist? Even a pathetic "How are you?" Unlike the blonde, I can't come up with clever, teasing remarks to make him laugh out loud, let alone smile. I can't come up with anything at all. I'm struck dumb.

But time out.

That's not an issue because he doesn't bother to even look back at me. He stares out, cold, self-involved, totally not interested. The wall is up, his message received. I turn away and make my way down to the water, throwing my sunglasses on the ground and running into the waves, swimming out deeper and deeper and deeper.

Over my head. Beyond saving.

twenty-one

I watch a ballet of sea turtles paddle by; hammerhead sharks cruising in slow, deliberate circles surrounded by an entourage of platinum fish like silver rain. The stony coral reefs are so close I run my hands over their scratchy surface, as hard and skeletal as jagged bone. I swim over forests of orange and yellow sea anemones as bright as summer fruits, their drunken feathery heads and spidery legs doing a quivery hula dance in the water.

Tufts of seaweed lightly stroke my face like grassy fingers. I stare up to the surface where the sunlight harpoons yellow shafts of light through the water. Only the brightness doesn't reach the bottom of the ocean floor. Down there, it's dark like the inky black of midnight: a cold, uninviting, distant world where predators hide in waiting.

He's in the water somewhere, swimming silently, stealthily getting closer and closer. Only there's no hint where, not a ripple on the surface. I see manta rays as wide and thick as fleshy carpets and wolf eels, soft and graying as evil-looking old men.

I want to call out to him, to reach him, only he isn't anywhere. I look all around and then I see him, or at least I think I do. He's way up above the surface, staring down at me. I try to call him, but I can't speak. I reach up to where he is to wave, only an army of weeds holds me back like a helpless fish wound up in a net. I slither out of their hold and rise to the surface searching for him, but I'm too late. He's gone.

The scorching white light of the sun steals my sight and all I can make out is an endless world of steel-blue water where I swim and swim and swim and never stop.

⸻

I wake up in a hot, sweat-soaked T-shirt, burning red eyes, and a throat with a razor blade inside it. I sit up and the earth shifts.

"Oh God."

Aunt Ellie brings me a thermometer. She puts her cool hand on my forehead. "You're burning up."

102 and a half.

She snaps into action. "Take these," she says, handing

me aspirins and then water. Then she reaches for the phone. "I'll call the doctor."

"He's coming to the house?" No doctor I saw ever did that. But this isn't a big city and Dr. Jenner is a friend. She calls him Craig.

"Some sort of virus," he says, shrugging slightly. My glands are swollen, but other than that, he says, "There's nothing remarkable." Translation: *Virus* means they can't pin it down. The good news is no gagworthy medicine.

"Sleep and drink lots of fluids," he tells me. "Call me in a few days if you don't feel better."

I'm not going to the beach for the rest of the century, so that's fine.

"Don't tell my parents." I plead with Aunt Ellie in a scratchy unrecognizable witch voice. "They'll only worry, and what can they do anyway?"

"Let's see how you do."

She knows I'm right, I can tell. When they call, I'll say I was out with some girls I met. They'll be happy to hear I'm making friends.

I don't want to watch TV and I can't concentrate, so books are out. I lie back in bed and stare at the lacy salt patterns on the windows and watch the gray sky darken. I drift into a sweaty, uneasy sleep, my wet shirt against my skin under the steamy blanket tent.

I wake up and stare at the alarm clock. Nine. Day or

night? Where am I? Then I remember. Something woke me, but what? My forehead's still hot and I reach for the water bottle next to my bed. It hurts to swallow, but I finish it and want more, but there's an entire flight of stairs to go down.

I lay back on the pillow and gaze out the window at hazy clouds over the moon. Somewhere in the heavens it sounds like metal curtains are shaking. Seconds pass and the sky ignites with Fourth of July fireworks. It happens again and again.

From somewhere behind me, the awful moans of the dead begin.

I don't have the strength to run down to Aunt Ellie so I pull the covers up to my face and lie there with my eyes squeezed shut. I cringe in fear as something cold, almost rubbery sweeps across my head—like icy fingers that make my scalp vibrate. Goose bumps spread all over my arms.

"Stop it!" I cry out trying to punching away in the dark. "HELP."

I cover my head with the blanket and it gets so hot I can hardly breathe. I lie still, but the feeling starts to creep up my spine again. It's like being on a dark street and knowing something's there and it's reaching out and touching you, only you can't see anyone or anything, you just feel the touching and you're powerless to stop.

"Stop it," I cry out. "Stop it."

Then I sit up and there it is.

A quivering mask of a face floats in the air and stares back at me. There are burnt-out holes where the eyes should be. A head, but no body, floating in the air, floating. It swoops near me and then drifts back and then that awful moaning builds up again that I can feel in my bones.

"What do you want? Why are you here?" My throat is so sore I can barely get the words out.

It makes that awful, inhuman squeal again like it's sick or in agony. The sound rakes through me and I shiver and then break out in a cold sweat.

Behind me, the staircase begins to squeak.

"Who's there?" I scream without a voice.

"Sirena?"

"Aunt Ellie, God, you scared me to death."

She sits at the side of my bed.

"The ghosts..." I whisper.

"Poor you," she says, leaning over and hugging me. Then she puts the back of her hand against my forehead. "A double whammy."

She hands me a thermometer and I put it in my mouth. It beeps and I look down. Now it's 101 degrees.

"Progress," she says, handing me more aspirins. "Do you want something to eat? I made you chicken soup."

I shake my head.

"Just a little? It will help your throat."

"Later."

"What about company?" The futon opens to a bed. She's willing to stay, maybe to help me ward off the ghosts.

"It's okay, I'm fine now."

She raises her eyebrows. "Really?"

Still she sits with me and we watch nothing on TV, channel surfing, only we can't find anything remotely interesting except local news and then an old black-and-white movie that's supposed to be funny. Eventually Aunt Ellie clicks off the TV. The stairs groan as she goes down.

The rain taps lightly against the window now. The lightning and thunder have stopped. I'm almost asleep except for the barest shadow at the foot of my bed. I roll over and close my eyes.

For now, at least, it's quiet.

twenty-two

If I had a diary, it would be filled with my rants and frustrations about the incomprehensible way people act in this world. There would be volumes two and three. My misery trilogy.

But I never wanted a diary because sooner or later I'd forget to lock it and my parents would end up seeing everything because I'd leave it open on my bed. That left me with a snake pit of thoughts in my head.

Marissa would now think I was bipolar. Or had sunstroke. One day I was mailing her drawings of someone with movie-star looks who had the noble profession of saving lives. The next I was slamming him, the two-faced snake.

"He's inhumanely cold and unfeeling. Tear up the drawing, or better yet, burn it. The stupid blonde can have him." I stashed Antonio's painting at the bottom of my suitcase, facedown.

141

Hey Marissa,

I now know it's pointless to even think about liking anyone, ever. If you do, you doom yourself to misery and complete despair. Although if you happen to be a goddess with waist-length hair and a body like a fitness instructor, maybe that's not the case. Then life offers you everything you could dream of and more. The most frustrating thing is, I can't figure out what I did to deserve getting snubbed, but clearly there was something that turned me into a bottom feeder in his eyes. I want to ask him what. I do. I really want to know; only I'd never humiliate myself that way and give him the satisfaction.

You don't know how much I wish I was away in the mountains with you. Life makes sense there. It's normal and predictable and even boring is better than this. There's a regular schedule, things to do and yes, I'd welcome the stupid pranks we used to play on everyone. But most of all, I'd have friends in the bunk—especially you!

Write soon—no, sooner.

Love,

Sirena

twenty-three

God, Sirena,

I totally cannot figure out what happened. I wish I had been with you, so I could have seen his face and the look in his eyes. Does he have a gigantic attitude now because you nearly drowned? Does he blame you? Is he annoyed that he had to go out after you? That's so ridiculous. Really, that's what I altogether hate about boys. They're never direct. They never tell you what's on their minds. You have to pry it out of them or spend huge amounts of time trying to figure out their stupid Rubik's Cube brains, and really in the end, they seem to actually think and feel much less than we do, so overall you totally wasted all that time and effort.

Things here are interesting. So on-again-off-again Geoff definitely seems to like me now. I like him back, except for the teeth thing, which is totally obsessive and obnoxious, I know, but I can't help it. (At least teeth are something you can fix, right?) Can't *believe the summer is half over. Glad your swimming is getting better and you're spending time doing art. You will definitely win a scholarship to wherever you want to go. Write immediately and try to keep it together!*

Love,

Marissa

⚜

I have to get out of the house. It's been over a week and while my mind isn't normal, my temperature has been for two days straight. I need to go back to the hospital—or at least someplace else—because I'm going insane from boredom.

"Give it another day or so," Aunt Ellie says. "You won't be helping anybody there if you go back before you're completely over it."

So I take my sketchbook and walk to the beach. I'll hide myself in some quiet part far from where he is so he'll never know I'm there. I'm glad to be outside anyway, even though the water is rougher than usual because of the thunderstorm.

I cross the street to the beach and stop. Something is weird. It's quiet and empty. It's a perfect day, so why isn't anyone on blankets and chairs, the way they usually are? This makes no sense. Where is everyone?

That's when I spot a crowd down at the edge of the

water. An alarm sounds in my head and my heart goes into panic mode. I turn to the lifeguard chair.

It's empty.

I drop my things and run down to the water, easing my way through the crowd. A man is stretched out on the beach. Pilot's crouched over him, his yellow hair curtaining the man's face as Pilot compresses his chest and then does mouth-to-mouth breathing.

"What happened?" I whisper to a girl standing next to me.

She shrugs. "Nobody knows if the guy just swam out too far or had like a heart attack or something."

From somewhere behind me, a tall, balding man with a gut elbows his way through the crowd, head high.

"I'm a doctor," he announces, striding over to Pilot, waving him away. Pilot holds up a hand, but the doctor wants to take over. "Did anyone call an ambulance?"

Pilot stops and turns to him. "They're on their way." He stands up and steps back, letting the doctor take over. It looks like he's doing the same things Pilot did, leaning over him, breathing into his mouth, then pushing down on his chest with one hand over the other.

The doctor stops and looks up at Pilot. He asks for something that sounds like a defib.

"We don't have one," Pilot says.

The doctor turns back to the man. "C'mon," he says,

as if he's impatient with him. "Breathe." He tries again and again, but the man lies there motionless, his skin waxy and pale, one arm outstretched in a helpless gesture. I stare at him, waiting for him to stir. The doctor reaches up and places his fingers on the side of the man's neck. He shakes his head and gets to his feet. "He's gone."

Pilot looks back at him silently. He squats down. "Let me try for a few more minutes."

The doctor turns to in disbelief. "He's *gone*," he says again. He turns to the crowd holding up his hands.

"Back off, please," he says. "Show some respect." He turns and steps a few feet away.

Pilot ignores him, beginning the artificial respiration again, trying over and over. The doctor shakes his head and then turns and walks away.

But Pilot goes on, consumed, as if he refuses to accept death. I'm filled with pity for him, at the same time struck by his desperate, repeated attempts and his insistence to keep fighting and fighting, not giving up even when there's obviously no hope at all. Almost methodically he keeps trying to get air into the dead man's lungs, then he compresses his chest. "Breathe," I hear him whisper imploringly. "Breathe."

The man doesn't budge.

How long is he going to keep this up?

Finally he crouches closer and presses his forehead

against the man's chest. I watch in fascination as he places his hands around the man's head as though he's trying to bring some life force from his own body into the man's skull. I'm hypnotized by his movements, the intensity in his face, the energy I can almost feel that he sends out from his body. I've never seen anything like this before. I've never seen anyone like *him* before. I don't understand it all, but something about it makes me afraid. I forget where I am as I watch this healing rite, or whatever it is, without taking my eyes off Pilot.

I'm unable to turn away from him. I watch in wonder, filled with the oddest sensation that I'm witnessing something surreal, outside of myself that I can't take in. What I'm seeing is unknowable, my mind says, which makes no sense.

Most of the crowd has turned away and gone back to their chairs, their books, their music, the drama over. But I stay locked in place.

What is he doing? Praying? Chanting? His eyes are closed. He's breathing hard. I hear a humming sound like an energy force from deep inside him. His face is flushed, his forehead and upper lip glistening with sweat. He's talking to the man or communicating with him in some unspoken way, but his lips don't move. Next he's blowing at the man's head. He's so intense, so animated, I expect smoke and mystical visions to fill the air around him as if this is an ancient healing rite, something Antonio would know from his father, the rainforest shaman, the healer who Antonio swears could cure cancer and save people close to death. My eyes are fixed on him and out of nowhere what takes shape before me is otherworldly. A white, opaque mist or cloud of some sort rises up between the man and Pilot. I rub my eyes to make sure it's not something clouding my own vision, or a puff of cloud from the moist ocean air. This isn't the Amazon. He's not a rainforest healer.

Nothing in front of my eyes makes sense.

He works on the man more and more. How long before he lets go, before he gives up? I keep watching, powerless to turn away, but for his sake, I don't want to be seeing his desperate efforts to defy death. I force myself to look away. I focus on a broken pink sea shell at my feet, a smooth piece of blue sea glass in the sand glistening in the sun.

From the corner of my eye there's a flash of movement.

Was I imagining it?

I look up again. The man hasn't moved. He's lying there, dead.

I imagined it.

Only a moment later his chest seems to rise. A leg jerks. Seconds later his head turns to the side and he begins to cough. Pilot slides a hand behind the man's neck and lifts his head as water pours from his mouth.

"Jesus, did you see that?" somebody behind me yells. "HE'S ALIVE!"

My mouth opens and closes without a sound. Whatever just happened here in broad daylight eclipsed normal, everyday life.

The loud wailing of a siren drowns out all other sound as an ambulance screeches up. The back doors are flung open hard. Two EMS techs run toward us with a stretcher.

"He's breathing now," Pilot says, immediately composed, wrapped in a veil of calm. He's back from wherever he was. He's the lifeguard again, just a person who works at the beach pulling people out of deep water.

Word spreads across the beach. "What's going on?" I hear a voice shout. I turn and see the doctor running back to Pilot. "What's going on?" he repeats.

"He's breathing," Pilot says, lifting his chin. The faintest glimmer of triumph crosses his face.

The doctor studies him and shakes his head, the color leaching out of his skin. "What in the world did you *do*, man?"

twenty-four

I haven't seen Antonio since I was sick. He's my anchor. I've missed talking to him. I let Aunt Ellie know where I'm going and I bike to his favorite patch of beach. When I spot him he turns and waves. I think we share a sacred connection.

"Sirena," he calls out in his deep, musical voice. "Are you better?"

I go over and sit in the sand by his feet. "Yes." *How did he know?*

Edna catches my eye and I smile at her. That's all the encouragement she needs. She rolls onto her back.

Antonio peers into my eyes, making his own diagnosis.

"Did Aunt Ellie tell you I was sick?"

He shakes his head. "Pilot."

"How did *he* know?"

Antonio shrugs. "I suppose from people in the hospital?"

I look at him skeptically, but he turns and lifts his brush, concentrating on making short, fine strokes on the paper, filling in the white space.

Maybe Pilot was modeling for him again and while he was posing Antonio asked about me. I don't ask too much. I don't want to seem like I'm obsessed with him.

"So how did you get sick, Sirena?"

"How?" I shrug. "I just did...I woke up that way. I caught a virus from someone in the hospital, I guess. I really don't know."

"Sometimes we make ourselves sick," Antonio says. "It's our body's way of expressing what's inside our heads."

He doesn't look at me when he says this. Does he know what happened? How could he? Did Pilot tell him how he completely blew me off?

Antonio keeps painting.

⁓◦⌒◦⁓

My first day of kindergarten, I can't forget it. I was so nervous that after breakfast I threw up. It happened the next day too. Then I think of the headaches.

I start telling Antonio about them and my voice won't stop.

151

"There's something else..." I hesitate and look over at him.

"Go on," he says, gently.

I rub the heel of my hand back and forth along the sand, smoothing it, like the runway for a toy plane. I look up and begin to tell him all the things I never told anyone else before, not even Marissa.

"One day last year I was coming home from school. I was driving and I was alone in the car."

He listens closely, I can tell, because of how he holds his head and the way his eyes look out ahead of him, so serious.

"I was supposed to go bowling, only our regular place was closed for a private party, so the team agreed to meet someplace else, about five miles away in another part of the city, a place I usually don't go to." I stop and stare out at the waves smashing against the shore and at how behind them, if you look out farther, you see new ones rising up to take their place.

"Please," Antonio says, inviting me to continue.

"I was on the freeway...There wasn't much to look at, just signs, cars, and then off to the side of a road... a small motel."

He shifts in his chair, turning to me. He places his paintbrush down in the narrow slot on the easel.

"I don't know why, but right away my eye picked out a truck in the parking lot of the motel. It was instantaneous, a kind of déjà vu. Without thinking, I got off at the next exit and drove back to the parking lot. I knew then why the car looked so familiar. Even though it was a pickup—the same black Ford pickup that everyone in the universe drives— it had one thing that made it different. Someone had dented the door and scraped off the paint, and it hadn't been fixed yet."

"*Querida*," Antonio whispers.

"So...it was...my father's truck."

I swallow hard and stare back at the waves. The sun is slowly sinking lower in the sky, getting ready to hide for the night. I take in a breath. I need more air. "I sat in the parking lot and an uneasy feeling spread through me."

Antonio looks at me with such compassion that my eyes fill with tears. He sits silently, watching me. "I don't know how long I waited in the parking lot, but when it got close to supper time, I started to pull out."

He shakes his head slightly.

"As I was leaving, I looked in my rearview mirror. He was coming out of one of the rooms. He was with a woman. His arm was around her waist. She was young, so much younger than him."

"Sirena," he whispers, like an apology.

"Maybe we do get sick for a reason."

We sit for a long time, neither of us speaking. Antonio paints, and I watch him. The air gets cooler as the sun starts

153

to disappear. It's almost dark when he finally puts down his paint brush.

"Are you okay to get home by yourself?"

I nod. "Thanks for listening, Antonio."

"I'm your *friend*, Sirena," he says. He reaches out and covers my hand in his.

I get to my feet finally and start to walk back to my bike. I feel stripped of body armor. It's the same hurt as the day I saw him. I want to ask Antonio if there's a special plant or medicine in the Amazon jungle, some pill or magic drink that I can swallow. Something that's strong enough to make the pain go away forever, along with the memory. Before I get on the bike I stop and walk back to him. "Did you hear about the man who almost drowned today?"

He nods.

"I was there...Pilot saved his life. I never saw anything like that, Antonio. There was a doctor there who tried to save him, but he gave up. If Pilot didn't keep working on him he would have died. I think he *did* die, but..."

Antonio's face breaks into a smile. "He's good, he has learned."

"What do you mean?"

"He is the keeper of the flame. The human spirit."

I pretend to understand.

Aunt Ellie looks worried when I walk into the house. "I thought you'd be back earlier."

"When I talk to Antonio, I lose track of time."

"Well at least call, please."

She's a science writer, so I ask her something that's been bothering me.

"Aunt Ellie...is Antonio psychic or something?"

She tilts her head to the side. "How do you mean?"

"Sometimes I get the feeling he knows things before they happen...or...I don't know...he *sees* things."

"I'm not sure," she says. "What I do know is that he sees more than most of us. And understands more. He's got this..."

She searches for the right word. "Depth."

"He said Pilot's a 'keeper of the flame.' What did he mean?"

"He's a *lifeguard*," she says. "Literally."

"What do you mean?"

"He saves people...except for..."

"For what?"

"Nothing," Aunt Ellie says impatiently, getting up and going to the kitchen. "That was a long time ago."

twenty-five

Aunt Ellie dangles a crystal charm on a thin gold chain in front of me. It looks like a fist clenched for victory.

"Antonio dropped this off for you."

"What is it?"

"It's called a figa," she says. "It's a good luck charm from Brazil that dates back to African myths from the seventeenth century. It attracts positive energy, they say, and protects you from evil. But it has to be a gift to work, Antonio said."

I fasten the tiny clasp behind my neck and look in the mirror. "So now nothing bad can happen to me—ever."

She purses her lips. "I'm not sure it's *that* good."

<hr>

I don't usually go out alone at night. But the air is cooler now and I need to get out and run. The screen door bangs shut behind me and I sprint toward the beach. The ocean glows with an eerie yellow haze from the full moon.

I keep going for a few minutes, slow down, then sprint again. Finally I kneel at the edge of the water to wet my face and arms and cool off. Above me is an endless expanse of night sky. I listen to my own breathing and the lapping of the waves—the only sounds in the uncut stillness that surrounds me like a blanket of darkness.

I get to my feet and tighten my shoelaces. I stretch then take off again, building to a steady pace. My breathing is easier, I'm in better shape. I keep going, happy this outdoor world is mine alone.

Then out of nowhere, it isn't.

I'm overcome with the odd sensation that someone else is out there, nearby. I look around me. Nothing stirs. No one makes a sound. I slow my pace.

"Hello?"

No answer and I feel silly. It could be a fluttering bird or small animal, something that belongs here more than I do. The tiny flash of a firefly dances by. Another sparkle to my left. Another past my ear. I swipe it away.

It's safe to be on the beach at night. It is. This isn't a big city, there's hardly any crime.

Still...

Is my street sense forever on alert or am I just paranoid?

The boom of male laughter in the distance shatters the quiet. I jump. It's the kind of laugh that comes with too many beers. I flash to the poker games that went on too late when my father had his friends over. I would lie in bed listening, waiting for them to go home.

More laughter. This time like a crash of thunder. There could be a beach party nearby or a group out on a deck. I keep walking and then start to run toward home, anxious, on alert, but I keep going, determined not to let myself get overcome by fear—fear of nothing.

You're not used to being outside, by yourself, I tell myself. It's all in your head.

Only it isn't.

There's something on the sand ahead of me.

As I get closer, I make out the outline of a figure. I keep going and see that a guy of forty or more is lying with his head back, his long, tangled black hair coated with sand. He's drunk and revolting, his shirt half open, twisted around him. He has a thick, hairy chest.

"Hey," He raises a bottle of beer toward me. "Wanna drink?" He's slurring his words.

I shake my head and run.

"Hey, wait, wait."

I run faster and faster, my breath coming so hard it aches. I lose track of where I am or how far I've gone, until it feels safe to relax and cool off. I slow to a walk, fixated with watching the water. Off in the distance I spot someone at the edge of the waves.

Don't get freaked out, I tell myself.

And I don't.

Disconnect. Out of context.

I slow, but my heart doesn't. It's the perfect, chiseled profile I recognize first. Instead of board shorts, he's wearing a white T-shirt and jeans. Nervousness rises up in me. Why would he be here at this hour? Is he with someone? Did I interrupt something? I keep walking toward him. I have no choice.

"Pilot," I blurt out.

"Sirena."

"What are you doing here?"

He looks at me quizzically. "What do you mean?"

"You're not on duty, are you?" I say lightly.

"I come out here at night sometimes. What about you?"

I shrug. "I wanted to exercise and, you know, get air." I hesitate. "There's some crazy drunk down there." I point behind me.

He nods. "I know him, he's harmless."

He looks at me and comes closer. "I'll walk you back."

"You don't have to."

"I know."

I want him to, but I don't. Can you feel two conflicting

emotions at once? Anxiety balls up in my stomach. The harder I try to be as calm as he is, the worse it gets, the tension doubling back on me. There's the wall, the awkwardness. I'm captive in this uneasy world when he's near me. I'm never prepared for him.

Why did you ignore me? I want to ask him. Do you know how I felt? Do you know how much it hurt? Only I have to stop those kinds of thoughts. What would be the point? We walk along without talking, the silence creating a wider divide. Help! I want to scream out to nobody and everybody. How ridiculous is that?

Should I say something about the man he rescued? Anything I can think of will sound like I'm in awe of him and what he did. So I don't, which makes no sense, even though for him, bringing someone back from the dead may be nothing unusual.

I stare up at the sky hoping for an opening line. It's flecked with a million stars.

I try *not* to think of what an impossibly perfect setting this is.

I try *not* to think that he's *not* thinking of what an impossibly perfect setting this is.

I pretend to concentrate on hunting for the few constellations I recognize. He must be wondering what to say too because after a few minutes he lifts his chin toward the sky. "Full moon," he says.

"What do you think is going to happen?"

"More murders, accidents, suicides, births, kidnappings."

"Really?"

He laughs softly and shakes his head. The rare smile. "No."

⁓⦿⦿⁓

So he gets over on me, but his nearness blurs my vision like the wrong glasses. Things don't appear the way they're supposed to. Is there a breathalyzer test for emotions that shows if you're off balance and out of touch with reality? It feels like we're two distant planets and I'm orbiting around him in slow motion.

He kneels and picks up a stone, skimming it above the water. Plop, plop, plop, it lands exactly the way it's supposed to.

What is he not good at?

A gauzy haze veils the moon as we walk on. "How long have you been a lifeguard?

"Three years."

"Have you ever *not* saved someone?"

He looks away for a moment, then turns back to me. "Once," he says, softly. "Myself."

"What do you mean?"

"I was out on a swimming practice with some other

161

guys, and all of a sudden we were surrounded by dolphins. They herded us together and wouldn't let us swim away. "

"That's so strange."

"We thought so, too. Then we saw why."

"What was it?"

"There was a great white shark nearby, and they wouldn't let it come near us. They were protecting us, we realized, the way they protect their own.

"What happened then?"

"They surrounded us until finally the shark swam away. Then they broke the circle and let us swim back to shore."

"That's extraordinary."

"I know."

"Things like that must happen to you all the time."

He reaches for my arm, disturbed. "Why do you think that?"

"Because you're not *like* anyone else."

"Neither are you."

"You know what I mean."

"Do I?"

I start to turn away, and then turn back and face him again. "What *is it* with you? Why do you *hate* me?"

He reaches for my shoulders and pulls me toward him, a tiny muscle quivering in his cheek. "Is that what you think?"

"Yes."

"I don't hate you," he says, his face so close I can almost feel the warmth of his skin. He waits, not moving, then abruptly pulls back, dropping his hands. "I...I'm sorry. I shouldn't have..."

"Shouldn't have what?"

He shakes his head sinking into silence. He's off somewhere in his head.

I walk off ahead of him, wincing from the lost opportunity. What is it? His girlfriend, the blonde? He obviously doesn't feel he needs to explain anything to me. Some girls wouldn't let him get away with that. They'd be up front, direct. *Afraid to make a move because of what your girlfriend would say?*

Only I can't.

I turn to stone and look back at him. "It totally doesn't matter, okay?" It comes out in a rush, with more annoyance and frustration than I want to show, only I can't hide the anger building in me. "I have to get going, my aunt will start worrying." I start running ahead.

"Sirena, wait."

I keep going, faster now, only his legs are longer and he catches up, reaching for my arm. "Stop, please."

I look up at him and want to stamp my feet. He's calm on the outside but below the surface he's deceptively deep and unknowable.

Like a riptide.

"I don't hate you," he insists. "I don't want you to think that."

"Why do you *care*?"

He runs the back of his hand lightly down the side of my face. I swallow hard, leaning in to him, my insides aching with some primal longing. I press my lips into the side of his neck inhaling his sweetness like a narcotic. I shouldn't, I know it, only I'm powerless to stop myself. I lift my face up to his until our lips meet. I don't care anymore, I don't. I'm desperate to kiss him

Only he stands there stoically, emotionless, cold, his eyes shut.

He doesn't kiss me back.

"It won't work," he says, "and I don't want to hurt you."

Am I that pathetic?

I stand back and shake my wrist loose of his grip. "I won't give you the chance."

I turn and run back to the house, tears streaming out of my eyes. His words echo in my head, slicing into me like a knife. At least now I know for sure how he feels and I can't pretend anymore. He's completely cold to me, he doesn't care in the least. I've been living in my own blind fantasy world.

I hate you, I want to scream. But it's my fault for what

I did. I started it. I brought it on. What a desperate and pathetic loser I must seem to him. I run faster and faster, filled with fury.

This time he doesn't call after me...and he doesn't follow.

twenty-six

DANGEROUS RIP CURRENTS:
STAY OUT OF THE WATER.

The signs are everywhere, posted all along the fencing near the beach. I look out.

Not a soul is in the water anywhere.

All over the sand, beachgoers are trying to cool off by sitting under umbrellas, fanning themselves and downing cold drinks. I don't have an umbrella and I've finished every drop in my quart-sized water bottle. I lay out on my blanket, staring up at the sky, the sun blistering my skin.

I hate Pilot. I hate him, I hate him. I hate him. I blame him for the riptides. I blame him because I'm roasting. It's over ninety-nine degrees and I'm stuck in the middle of a beach with nowhere to swim and nothing to do and no one to do anything with. I'm in a total sweat and so furious I feel like screaming. It's his beach, or at least he acts like it is, so it's all his fault and I'd like to strangle him.

I hate his superiority, the uncomfortable way he makes me feel, the way he sets you up as if he's interested and the next moment gives you the deep freeze, disabusing you of the laughable notion that someone like you might hold even the slightest appeal to him.

If that wasn't bad enough, the rejection came on top of the news that my parents—so busy house hunting and splitting up—weren't even planning to visit me this summer.

"Money is very tight, Sirena," my mom said. "You have to understand that, baby." Why did I have to understand everything about them? Why didn't anyone understand what *I* was going through?

My life sucks. Plain and simple. And it's not like there's anything on the horizon to make it better. I look at my skin turning red. Screw sunblock. I bury it in the sand. What does it matter if I burn? Who cares about skin cancer?

Out of the corner of my eye I watch him high up in his chair looking out at the beach and down on everyone. He's not in a sweat. Maybe he's cold now, instead of hot because he's not like everybody else or *anyone* else. His face isn't beaded with perspiration. How is that possible? Does he have a supernatural cooling mechanism so he doesn't sweat, just like he doesn't bruise? Maybe he doesn't even sunburn; he only tans and the color automatically stops when he's a divinely toasty brown because of his internal perfection meter.

Eventually he makes his way to the sand and walks off. He's on foot patrol now, wandering all along the beach as if to let people know he's there, that he's watching. I keep my eye on him until he's almost out of my field of vision.

Slowly I make my way to the pier, just outside the swimming area. I sit at the edge, watching the water. It doesn't look particularly dangerous to me. Wouldn't you be able to see riptides if they were really there? Wouldn't the water look wild, wouldn't the waves look bigger and fiercer than they do now?

Three girls pass by in low-cut bikinis. They put down a blanket, drop a pillow-sized bag of cheese doodles and a six-pack of Diet Coke and lay out in the sun. One is tall and thin, almost gaunt. She must live on Diet Coke. Her hair is long and dark in ringlets. The other two are blondes, closer to my age. They laugh constantly like there's absolutely nothing in the world that isn't funny. They must be in a sorority because they're all wearing identical silver charm bracelets with dangling hearts.

"So I asked him to come to the party," one of the blondes says.

"Get out. Pilot?"

My ears perk up.

"Duh, yes."

"What did he say?"

She laughs and raises an eyebrow. "He's definitely coming."

"*I* want him," the other one says, kicking the friend.

"Bitch, I saw him first."

"*Who gets the hot lifeguard, who gets the hot lifeguard?*" the first one singsongs, then cracks up.

The brunette grabs the bag of cheese doodles. She whacks it with the heel of her hand and it bursts open with a boom, shooting cheese doodles out over the sand. That's the funniest thing in the world to them.

Nausea washes over me and my head pounds. I'm on the brink of madness. If I had just one person to talk to, one living soul who could understand this.

I don't care about anything anymore.

I stand up.

I'm going in.

I won't go in all the way. That would be dumb. I'll wet my feet and hands, duck down fast and come out. I'll cool off, not die of heatstroke. What big harm could come from that?

I turn my head to the lifeguard's chair. Still empty.

I take baby steps into the water, immediately aware of a strange and exciting drawing sensation as the water swirls crazily around my toes and they sink into the wet sand. It's an odd, tickling feeling, as if gravity is trying to draw me out to the center of the earth. My toes disappear as though I've stepped into quick sand. I smile—this is a test I hope to ace.

Sirena against the odds.

Another baby step.

One more. The water's just below my knees.

No big deal.

I splash water over me and then wet my face. Yes, I'm finally cool. I look down and watch the way the water changes my bikini from pale to deep green like it has magical powers. Before I turn to go back out, I take one more step forward. The bottom deepens unexpectedly as if I've stepped into a hidden crater. I try to step back but I lose my bearings. I topple forward, the pebbly sand scraping my knees.

"Ow," I cry out, then I turn, embarrassed. Did anyone hear me? The three girls are gone now. Not many people are near me outside the swimming area by the pier. The few that are seem to be napping or lost in their own worlds, oblivious to everything but their favorite music. I manage to get back up on my feet. I take in a deep breath of relief. I turn and start to run out, back to the sand.

To safety.

But suddenly another strong wave rushes in, crashing

against the back of my legs. I'm thrown down again, angry, swirling water surrounding me. Then another wave. Only this time a rush of saltwater gets washed down my throat and I gag and start coughing as it chokes me. A sense of what's happening sends panic spreading through my insides like an electric current. Before I have a chance to try to get to my feet again, I feel a powerful, demonic force beneath me as though the ocean is intent on dragging me away to punish me for approaching it. I fight to step back to shallow ground again, to the dry sand only yards from where I am, but this time there's a stronger wrench and I'm dragged out farther and farther until the force of the tides drags me under the waves.

"Help," I scream, managing to poke my head over the surface. "Help." I throw my head back so I can breathe, but the water is pounding against me and it drowns out the pathetic squeal of my voice.

"Help," I yell out again before a torrent of water washes over me and I'm below the surface again. A deep bubbling sound fills my ears as I go down. Darkness surrounds me.

Where am I?

And then a low, rushing hiss as another swell of seawater engulfs me like a lasso. I reach out but there's nothing to take hold of. As I open my eyes, a clump of seaweed drops over my face like a blindfold, and boughs of driftwood caught in the currents rake my skin.

Where am I? Where am I?

When I rip away the seaweed, it dawns on me where I am, and terror tightens the back of my throat.

Buried under the pier, hidden from view.

No one can see me anymore. No one knows I'm here.

I'm scared, so scared, but I have to do something.

I look up and see dark planks of wood inches above my head, boxing me in, trying to bury me alive just feet below the surface of the ocean. I grope above me fighting the current, desperate to catch hold, to steady myself, only the wood is worn and rough and a thick splinter wedges itself under my fingernail like a spike, pain searing through me. I try to ignore it, choking back the burn as I fight against the water's force, trying to hold onto the wood above me to anchor me, praying for it to let up for just a few seconds so I can fill my lungs with air, just enough so I can try to call out again and keep fighting until someone spots me, but my arms are so thick and leaden with exhaustion and my heart slams so hard in my chest that I'm about to pass out.

And then, as if for no reason, the water seems to calm. I'm filled with hope. I can get out, now. I suck in as much air as my lungs can hold.

This is it.

My chance.

With every bit of strength I can summon, I begin to work my way out from under the pier, using both hands to hold the planks above me to keep me from going under, to steady myself. I manage to get almost to the end of it, close to the bright sunlight, and I exhale in a rush of giddy relief. I'm home safe, I'm free now. I can feel the sand under my feet again. Shallower water. I breathe in deeply, then again.

You're going to be okay, Sirena, I tell myself like a mother reassuring a terrified child.

I take one step, then another. But then my foot lands on something hard and rough that's sticking up like a mound in the sand.

A rock? What is it?

As I lift my foot to step away, it rears up and comes alive, a sea monster lying in waiting. It's as big as a blanket with horrible shiny, beady black eyes and it lashes into my leg viciously like a madman on the loose with a knife. Red heat scorches my insides.

"Help me," I scream before the pain fills my throat and all the fight and power leach out of me. A violent rush of water suddenly surrounds me, only now I'm powerless to fight it anymore. I sink down below the surface, watching the water around me darken from green to deep red to brown like the earth. I drop toward the rocky bottom and the world turns black and cold and goes achingly silent.

twenty-seven

When you're dying, people say you see a tunnel and a column of blinding light. Sometimes you can hear the voices of people around you, even though they don't know that you can. I remember a feeling of warmth and love, a kind I never experienced before. I gave myself over to a powerful entity, some great spiritual force in the universe as I floated without a body anymore, thinking about all of my life and my childhood. I saw my parents and grandparents and Aunt Ellie. I didn't have to talk to any of them, I couldn't, but it didn't matter because they were there with me in that wide expanse of white, enchanted space in a new sphere of existence somewhere outside the earth.

But then I approached an ending, or a border. I sensed an indistinct line in the sand between the worlds of life and death and I fought back hard, drawn by a strong lifeline. I crossed over to that other, more vivid, pulsating reality that I could see so clearly in my mind's eye, like a traveler crossing from one continent far away to another that was home. And then I floated, and slept, a deep calming sleep of renewal, rebirth, and completion.

⁓⊙⊙⊙⁓

The voices are behind me somewhere. I can't see anyone. There's a blinding light only this one is cold and white making everything ghostly and unnatural, hurting my eyes.

Where am I?

White sheets. A blanket. I'm in bed, only beeping sounds are everywhere.

A tape around my arm holds a needle attached to a tube. I hate needles; why is it there? Tiny droplets of blood, one after the other, trickle through the tube that goes inside me.

Why?

What happened?

What's wrong with me?

Why am I here?

I shift and a spasm of pain courses through my body. I can't move my left leg. It's dead, useless. Is it still attached? Am I paralyzed? I manage to move my arm. I push down the sheet. The leg is totally bandaged; only the dressing is

175

spotted with blotches of red and yellow. That's not right.

It's hard to focus, to think straight.

Am I drugged?

I can't remember anything. What happened to my mind? Who's talking behind me? I can't see anyone.

I force my eyes to open. The light burns. I make out the outline of someone in white. A nurse? She comes toward me and pours something from a small envelope, like a sugar pack, into a bag of watery liquid that's hanging on the pole with the blood.

"What is that?"

"A sedative...to help you sleep."

"Sleep?" It comes out muffled like there's cotton in my mouth—or my head. Have they fogged up my brain? "I don't want to sleep. I want to get up. I want to go home."

She shakes her head. "You need to rest, Sirena."

"Why, what happened?"

She doesn't hear me or pretends not to.

"What happened?" I repeat. Is she deaf? Why doesn't she answer?

She studies the monitor that's bleeping and writes something on paper on a clipboard. I want to ask her something else, but what? I can't focus. I can't think. Then I look up. Aunt Ellie comes toward me. She doesn't look like the Aunt Ellie I remember. Her face is gray and sad and pinched. She's older now. She looks scared. For the first time I see lines between her eyes. She reaches out for my hand and squeezes it. She pretends to smile, but it's hard for her. She's like that, she's honest. I feel pity for her, but I'm not sure why. A doctor walks in and studies a chart. His face is pale, lined, and emotionless. A nurse stands next to him with the same lifeless expression.

"What happened to me?" I ask everyone and no one.

"You were in the water and got swept out," Aunt Ellie says.

"How...how did I get here?"

"Pilot," she says.

It scares me to look at them. I break into a sweat, only I can't tell whether it's fear or fever. All I can focus on is the fire inside my leg. It's hot and throbbing. Then I hear voices from outside, in the corridor.

My eyes start to close, but I fight sleep. I try to make out the voices, I have to; I have to know what they're saying because all I know is it's about me. They're whispering about me, like ghosts from someplace else. Where was that? I try to remember. I hear sounds and words outside, behind me, but nothing is clear.

"Sirena," I hear. A voice cracks. There's crying. Something terrible has happened, my mind tells me. They're hiding it from me. They don't want me to know. Goose bumps spread up and down my arms. I'm cold, then hot. I can't tell which. Something terrible, something

177

terrible has happened, only what?

Terror spread through me, only I don't know why. It's what's *not* being said and how they're treating me. I'm not a sixteen-year-old girl anymore; I'm a number, a sad case that everyone is looking at with pity or not at all, averting their eyes because they don't want to show emotion. They don't want me to know what's happening.

Two people are arguing. One voice is higher, a woman's. I make out the words, "wait," then "heal." Then a man's voice, deeper and calmer, but insistent. There's only one word I can make out as my brain starts to succumb to the drugs and I sink back into nothingness, overpowered.

One word that plunges me into terror, like a knife through my heart.

Amputation.

❧

I wake up in semidarkness in a total sweat. Every inch of me is dripping, my gown soaked through. I shove off the blankets and then I'm shivering as if my body is trying helplessly to fix me, but doesn't know anymore what to do. It shifts gears from high to low and back again futilely as I break down. Sweat pours off me. My brain pounds. I have a fever, I know—like when my throat was red and I had the virus, only twenty times worse now.

I close my eyes and have fantasies of some horrible

sci-fi movie with a nurse holding a thermometer that says one hundred and ten. I put my hand against my forehead the way my mother used to when I told her I didn't feel well. It's burning, it's wet. My head pounds as if the brain tissues are on fire. I can't move. I'm paralyzed with pain. There's a curtain around my bed and machines with blinking monitors at my feet. Electronic bleeps and blips everywhere. What do they mean? Is someone watching what they show? Does anyone care? I'm not a person anymore, I'm a lab rat hooked up to give read outs that spell life or death.

WHAT'S GOING ON? I want to scream, as a deep, throbbing pain shoots through my leg.

In my delirium, some of what happened begins to come back to me...

⁓⊙⊱

The water, the pulling, fighting helplessly against the riptides. Something sliced away at me, a killing flood of pain. Did I die and come back? I start to cry and I can't stop. I want my mommy, my daddy, I don't have anyone here. Where are they? Where is everybody? Is there anyone in the entire world who cares about me? Why did they leave me all alone here—to die?

"Aunt Ellie," I call out for no reason.

No answer.

179

"Aunt Ellie," I call again to hear the sound of my own voice, just to let myself know I'm alive and I can still speak.

Still no one answers.

I have to get out of here. I have to go home. I want everything to stop because this is all wrong. I don't belong here, this isn't me. But my parents...I remember then. They're so far away, back in Texas. Do they even know I'm here? All they know is that they're getting divorced; they're separating and splitting up the family. And now they'll have one less thing to worry about because I'll never make it home again to see them, if they care at all.

I lie back on the pillow and try to clear my mind, to focus on what happened, to get it straight in my head. Pilot took me out of the water, Aunt Ellie said that, but how, when? I didn't see him, he walked the other way. He walked away from me.

How could he have known? How did he find me?

I look up and a face appears out of darkness, like a ghost, like one of the ghosts from Aunt Ellie's house. Only it's not.

Pilot.

"Help me," I beg. He looks at me pityingly and doesn't answer. "Please, please."

He stands there silently. Is he real? He stares out at all the tubes and monitors around me, the quivering lines and bleeps that send out a electronic song of life or death.

Blood drips slowly into my arm.

He walks toward the bed and I look at his face. This isn't the Pilot I know anymore. I see something in his eyes that I've never seen before.

"What? What is it?"

"I should have known," he says. "I should have been there to stop you."

I look back at him bewildered. "How could you have known?"

He doesn't answer. He sits in the chair next to me and leans toward me, studying my face. My eyelids flutter. It's such an effort to stay awake, but I fight it. If I close my eyes I may never open them again. I reach my hand toward him.

"Stay."

<hr />

It's dark when I wake up. I feel along the side of the bed for the button to push. Where is it? Why isn't it here? Don't they want to help me? I need a nurse. Someone has to give me something to take away the pain. I search for it, crazed, and then the curtains part suddenly. The nurse doesn't look at me, she doesn't smile.

She's in ghostly white like a vision. Like...the angel of death.

"My leg...It hurts so much, I can't stand it."

"It's the infection," she says. She shakes her head.

"There was no controlling it, it spread so quickly. But we'll put you to sleep, you won't feel anything. Nothing at all."

"Put me to sleep? What are you talking about? I don't want to go to sleep. I want to go home."

"Lie still," she says. "It will be over quickly—you won't feel anything. You'll heal. You'll be fine." She writes something in the chart and turns to go. She turns back to me for an instant. "I'll be back with the gurney."

Sweat pours down my forehead now and my heart slams insides my chest as though it's rearing up and attacking me like my own body is the enemy. My temperature must be a hundred and six. All I know is I have to get out of this place, whatever it takes, no matter how much I hurt. I have to get away from this woman, this monster—otherwise they'll cut me apart and kill me.

I rip the monitors off my chest and yank the tape from my arm and tug the needle out. Blood starts to spurt out of the opening, dripping onto the floor of the room like there's a purple geyser spurting from inside me. I lean up in bed and an excruciating wave of pain spreads over my entire body.

"I'M DYING," I scream out. "HELP ME, OH MY GOD, SOMEONE HELP ME." But if a God is in this room, he's silent, not showing his face. "HELP ME," I shriek again.

The curtains are pulled open sharply and the nurse is

back with two others now.

"Oh God," one of them says, looking at me. My hospital gown is soaked with blood. It looks like I was shot. I remember Cody's father and the way he looked.

"She's got to be sedated," someone hisses. I hear the word "psychotic." They lift me up and put me on a steel gurney, tying my hands to the railings so I can't move.

"WHERE ARE YOU TAKING ME?" I scream.

"It's okay," someone says.

I'm wheeled into the corridor, the blood still dripping from my arm. "NO," I yell out, "PLEASE."

We get to a pair of double doors with small glass windows and a sign over them:

Operating Room. No Outside Visitors Permitted.

The doors spring open and the gurney is pushed through. The doors close behind us. There's an enormous light in the room over a table. Everything's white like a blinding nightmare. On a table next to me there's a tray covered with a starched blue cloth. On top of it are dozens of pointed instruments, and razor sharp scalpels. What could they possibly do with so many knives?

"I didn't give my permission," I scream. They can't operate on you without your permission, I know that. "I DIDN'T SAY IT WAS OKAY," I scream at these stupid, horrible, deaf people who hear me but are intentionally ignoring me.

But before anyone can answer, there's a muffled B-O-O-M.

The lights are out everywhere.

From blinding operating room light, we're in total darkness.

"Blackout!" a voice from outside somewhere yells out.

"Why the hell didn't the backup generator kick in?" someone else screams.

"Get up to the control room," a voice commands. "This is an emergency." From somewhere behind me the gurney suddenly gets bumped and then pushed. I'm being rolled somewhere, but I don't know where. I hear the double doors of the OR flip open.

"Where are you taking me?" I call out.

But no one answsers.

"Where are you taking me?" I scream as loud as I can.

There's still no answer and I close my eyes, hoping my pounding heart won't burst through my chest as I get ready for my descent into hell.

twenty-eight

The rubber wheels beneath me continue to move quickly and silently down the corridor, bumping up and down as if we're going over thresholds on our way into rooms then out of them, going faster and faster, as if there's a definite destination where I'll end up.

Who's pushing me?

It's still pitch black out. As I pass doorways, slivers of moonlight shine through the windows. Is everyone sleeping? Am I the only patient aware of what's going on? In the distance I hear the scurrying of feet. Someone calls out something about a generator, the control room, but it's like background sound and I can't make it out. If my head didn't hurt so much I would turn back and look behind me, but I'm burning up and ready to pass out.

My leg is throbbing, only I don't think of that now.

I'm out of there, away from the bright lights, the blue tray with the steel instruments, the sharp knives, the hardware meant to slice people open and take out their insides and cut off their legs. Knives that can cut into your soul. And ruin your life.

Forever.

Something has changed, but what. Am I sleeping? Dreaming? Or dead? It feels like the atmospheric pressure is different and we're cruising over the clouds. I'm a balloon being filled with helium so I can rise and float over the universe. It's not as scary now. Nothing bad can happen to me. Has someone given me anesthesia? Am I going to sleep? What is it? What has changed?

Antonio? The figa?

Immediately I reach inside my hospital gown and buried inside it, around my neck, is the chain. I follow it until I reach the charm. Still there. They haven't taken it from me. They probably missed it.

I close my hand around it, and then I realize that my arms are free. When did that happen?

It feels like Antonio's near me. I knew he would keep me safe. It *was* him, or at least his power. He gave it to me, he helped me. Somehow he knew. Nothing bad can happen to me when I'm wearing it, when Antonio's watching out.

Do you hear my thoughts? Do you know what's happening? A silent voice inside my head asks him.

I feel myself smiling just before I slip back into unconsciousness.

⁓ↀ⁓

I stare out a window.

Night.

The moon. The hospital room, I'm back there again. My heart starts to quicken. Did I have the surgery? Machines are attached to me again and I jerk my head up. Oh God please, please, please, I don't want to spend my life in a wheelchair. I don't want to have one leg and have people pity me. I feel beneath the sheet and then I stare down and see my toes. All of them. I lie back again and exhale. Was it all a nightmare?

The soft blips of the machines are everywhere. Does that mean there's power again? Then I remember the blackout. People yelling out orders.

"Why didn't the generator kick in?" I heard someone say. "What if we were in the middle of the operation?"

I would have been dead.

I would have bled to death.

I rest my head back on the pillow. From behind me in the darkness something stirs.

"Who's there?"

Nothing.

Seconds go by and no one answers. I think of Aunt

Ellie's house, the ghosts. It couldn't be, please.

"Who's there," I say, louder. "Please." My voice cracks. Not the ghosts. I can't stand the idea of their moans, the damp fingers that reach out to touch me. I startle when a figure steps from the dark. A hand touches my shoulder.

"Me," he whispers. "Pilot."

He steps around to the side of the bed and looks down at me. He has a light beard and shadows under his eyes. The air around me seems filled with his sweet perfume.

"I'm glad you're here." I reach my arm out and he takes my hand in his. It's solid as the earth. "I'm glad you're here."

He smiles. "You already said that."

It must be the medicine. Or him. I can't think straight. He eclipses my sanity.

There's a chair next to the bed and I lift my chin toward it. "Sit, please." I study the way his dark, blue T-shirt outlines his lean, hard chest. He sinks down and leans back, closing his eyes, his hand tightly wrapped around mine. I watch his face. Is he asleep? As if in answer he opens his eyes. He looks at me and then turns and studies all the machines. Does he understand them? Can he read the patterns? He shakes his head slightly in disbelief.

"The day before yesterday you were sitting on the beach sketching..." he says, almost to himself, in a hoarse whisper.

"Do you know what happened to me?"

He looks at me and looks away.

"What?"

"You nearly drowned."

"Tell me what happened. Please. My mind's all muddled. I can't remember anything clearly."

He bites the side of his lip momentarily, but doesn't say anything.

"You saved me. It was you, right?"

He doesn't say no.

"I know it was. How did you find me? How did you know?" All I can remember is being angry at him. I wanted to swim and get cool. I'm overwhelmed with guilt for all the horrible, awful things I thought about him. All the blame. If he knew, he wouldn't look at me.

"You were calling, yelling out for help."

"But no one came. I thought I would die." I remember that now. "How did you hear me?"

"Sssshhh," he says, withdrawing his hand from mine. He leans over me and lightly places his hands over the blanket. I study the leather cuff that he wears wrapped around his wrist and realize for the first time that there's an animal tooth of some kind attached to it. But then I look closer. It's not an animal tooth—it's a figa. It made out of clear crystal—the exact duplicate of the one Antonio gave to me. I'm about to ask him about it when I feel a deep, comforting wave of warmth spreading over me, like stepping into a hot bath on a cold, winter day. He closes his eyes. Is he sleeping? Praying? He keeps his hands there and breathes harder as though it's an effort that takes all of his strength. I watch his jaw. His muscles tense. His hands reach up to the top of my head. Slowly, he begins to massage my scalp. He leans closer, his warm breath on my forehead.

And then a nurse comes in. She looks at him curiously.

He pulls back casually and looks up at her, wide-eyed, but there's a pulsing in his jaw.

"She has to get some sleep," she says. She shakes her head disapprovingly.

"I'll leave in a minute."

She stares at him, waiting.

"A minute," he insists, his jaw tense. He stares back, unflinching.

She walks out and his face relaxes. He leans over me again, touching my leg now and leaving his hands there. Is it my imagination, or do I feel the blood pulsing through his fingers as a healing energy seems to flow between us like an invisible transfusion of strength?

Only, that's crazy, it can't be.

He bows his head, finally dropping his head into his hands. He looks exhausted from the effort.

"What is it? What's wrong?"

"I'm so sorry. It was my fault."

"What was? You saved me."

"I should have known," he insists. He gets up and looks at me as though he's done something wrong, something he has to be forgiven for. "You don't understand, of course," he says, "but it's all right." He heads for the door. "I'll come tomorrow."

"Pilot, wait," I call, as the nurse comes in again.

"How did you know? I mean, I was under*water*, so how could you *hear* me?" He turns back to me, studying me for a few seconds.

"I hear your heart," he whispers, as he disappears through the door.

"What?" I say, almost to myself.

I look at the nurse, who's checking my IV. "Did he say what I think he did?"

She studies me curiously and shrugs. "He didn't say anything," she says. "Not that I heard."

twenty-nine

There's a yellow light behind my eyes, a warm light. I open them and see sunlight. It pours through the window and I squint. Was that what woke me? I lie back on the pillow. Something is different. But what? I'm stiff and uncomfortable. I shift and try to sit up.

Then I know.

The deep wrenching pain. It's gone.

The whole world feels flooded with sweetness and renewal. The impossibly blue sky that follows the darkest storm—a miracle like a green sprout that has burrowed its way through blocks of cement. Bad things wash away, the world turns and dark becomes light.

Someone thrusts a balloon bouquet into my hand and I look up. The hand that reaches out is my mom's. Next to her is my dad.

"Omigod!" My eyes flood with tears.

"Baby," my dad says, stepping toward me. He leans over and kisses my forehead. My mom sits down and hugs me. Tears stream out of her eyes.

"Don't cry, Mom, please, I'm okay."

"I know you are," she says, hunched over me, "but I was so scared." She stares out the window. I know what she's thinking, but she's wrong. It wasn't *her* fault, it had nothing to do with her. But I don't say anything. It's not the time to talk about what happened.

I look at them together. Is there a chance? Are they closer now because of what happened? But my dad's not putting an arm around my mom. They're next to each other, but they're not together.

"When did you get here?"

"Yesterday," my mom says. "Ellie called us as soon as it happened."

No one says anything.

It.

No one's exactly clear on *it*—not even me.

How much do they know? How much do *I* know? They're afraid to ask me anything, to upset me. They don't want me to talk about *it*. Unease washes over me, though. What if they want to take me home with them? I tackle it head on.

"I want to spend the rest of the summer here," I look

directly at my mom and then my dad. They can't say no to me now. I have the advantage. My dad stares at his feet. He doesn't know what to say.

"We'll do whatever's best for you," my mom says.

The nurse comes in, as if on cue. She's carrying my lunch tray. "Roast beef," she says, brightly. "Get it while it's hot."

It helps break the tension. My dad scratches the back of his head. "Do you serve parents?"

"They're not on the menu," she says, deadpan. Then she smiles. "There's a cafeteria downstairs."

I hear Aunt Ellie's voice outside. She's talking to someone else. "Four inches of rain," she says. "Half the state lost power."

I remember the OR and how everything shut off. What if there hadn't been a blackout, what would have happened to me? I'm also trying to figure out something else about the night, but Aunt Ellie comes over to my bed and puts a bouquet of daisies in a violet vase next to me and I forget.

"A still life," she says, with a half smile. "You can do a picture to brighten up the room. I brought your pencils."

The doctor comes in next with two medical students trailing him like baby chicks. His face lights up when he sees me now, the waxy mask of pity gone.

"Quite a turnaround, Sirena," he says, shaking his head. He lowers the blanket and gently lifts the tape on the bandage to show the students. We all stare at the foreign object that's my leg. There's a long, thin line where they stitched the gash, but the redness and infection are gone.

"She'll have full use of the leg," he says. He's bragging, as if he's the one the credit goes to. I shoot him a dark look that I hope his students will see. One of them is too busy taking notes, writing everything down, even when I sneeze. I guess he's preparing in case my leg and its fate will be the essay question on his final exam. When they all trail out, I try to swing my legs over the side of the bed, but it's impossible.

I surprise myself by finishing my entire lunch.

My dad smirks. "She never had a problem eating. Nearly had to take out a second mortgage on the place to pay the bills." My mom smiles. "That's not exactly the way I remember it."

My parents work hard at keeping the conversation going as if a dead space would draw us back to focusing on *it*. They must have vowed to do whatever had to be done for me and put all their feelings about each other out of the way. Still, their act is convincing. I push back the table with the empty plate.

"Aunt Ellie, is Pilot here today?"

She shrugs. "I'll ask." She jumps to her feet and leaves the room, probably glad I've given her something to do other than sitting with our sad party.

"Pilot?" my dad says.

"The lifeguard...The one who pulled me out."

"Why would he be here?"

"He's an EMS tech."

My parents exchange a glance that I'm not supposed to see. Just then Aunt Ellie comes back in. "He's at the beach, Sirena."

I look at all of them. "Then I have to go there—right now."

"What?" My dad looks at me in disbelief. He shakes his head, afraid to protest.

"Sirena, you're getting over a very serious accident," my mom says, gently. "I don't think they exactly want you going to the beach."

I look at my mom and dad and then Aunt Ellie. "If it hadn't been for him, you wouldn't have a daughter anymore."

They exchange glances without another word.

thirty

Dear Sirena:

What's up with you? I'm getting totally crazed!! You always write back and now, nada. Are you okay? Please tell me you are. I had all these scary dreams last night of you going out into the ocean and getting stranded out there. The Jaws thing, you know? Okay, that's stupid, but what else could I think? You're not mad at me, are you? I can't think of anything I did wrong. I'd call you if I could get to the damn phone, but you know how stupid they are about that here. Write soon and give me good news, okay? Jerko Geoff likes someone else, but it's not who I thought it was. She's a total rag. So what does that say about me?

Love you,
Marissa

Dear Marissa:

Oh God, BF, I'm so sorry I scared you. Actually I scared everyone here half to death, but I'm fine now, really. So much has happened that I don't know where to begin. Yes, I did almost drown. God, maybe you're psychic! But guess who got me out and saved my life?

I know you already know.

I'll never say another bad word about him for the rest of my life.

He's so much more complicated than I ever realized, I now know. He has these powers. It's...well...supernatural, or at least I think it is, if that's possible. It sounds crazy, I know, but lately it's turning out that everything in my world isn't what it appears to be on the outside and things are happening that I can't explain, and maybe I never will.

I'll write as soon as I know more, I swear. All is well here for now and that's all that counts. I feel reborn. How is that possible?

Love you so much,
Sirena

And ugh, so sorry about Geoff. Truthfully though, he never sounded like he was your type.

⤜◈⤐

No bikini now. A rumpled T-shirt over a denim skirt.

Far from beachside runway couture, but it's easy to slip on. I sneaked out of the hospital during the shift change in the only outfit that Aunt Ellie brought for me.

No attempt to cover the bandaged leg. Only now I'm not obsessed with my body anymore. All I care about is having a whole one. I could care less how I look compared to other girls.

Mark pushes the wheelchair and Aunt Ellie holds the crutches as our pathetic group slowly makes its way, first to the car and then the beach.

"This is insane," Mark says to Aunt Ellie, under his breath. She ignores him and I love her for that. I also love her for insisting that first, we drop my parents off at her house so they can take a break to shower and relax.

"We'll be fine," Aunt Ellie insists.

My iron-willed dad caves, to my surprise. My mom doesn't raise any objection either, which tells me that they're probably just totally burned out. I didn't realize they were up all night trying to get reservations, and then were forced to book indirect flights with long layovers because of bad weather. They must be dead.

I'm less than happy to go to the beach with an entourage. The cripple going to Lourdes, hoping to come away walking, cured, or in my case, less screwed up.

Mark turns into the parking lot and drives as close as he can up to the sand. I'm glad he doesn't have a dune buggy or he'd mow down the beachgoers to get on top of the lifeguard's chair. He parks, pops the trunk, and then heaves out the wheel chair, struggling to unfold it. It must weigh a thousand pounds, but he doesn't complain. He and Aunt Ellie help me get out of the truck and I hop over to the chair.

I don't know how I'm going to do it, I just know I have to, so I will. I'm grateful now that I went swimming and built up my arms. They push me as close as they can to the edge of the sand. Aunt Ellie hands me the crutches and I stand and tuck one under each arm.

Deep breaths.

Mind over matter.

You can control things if you set your mind to it. It takes practice to use them, I know. I remember once in school when a friend of mine broke her leg after skiing. She came in wearing a cast and used crutches to hobble to class. During lunch everyone took turns trying them out. I didn't realize how much it hurt under your arms to put all your weight on them.

I take a tentative step forward. Another. Is the whole world staring? It doesn't look that way. A few more steps and then, *whomp*, one of the crutches pitches forward and I topple over into the hot sand, landing hard on my hip.

"Shit," I mutter, scrambling to stand up. Mark runs over and helps me stand.

"You don't have to stand there watching me, for God's sake. Can't you just go for a drive or and come back later? I can get up by *myself*."

"Baby, this doesn't make any sense," he says, his voice insistent, imploring. "Do you want me to carry you?"

"Go home, Mark. I can do it, just give me a chance."

He looks back at Ellie, who waits by the car and nods. Outward Bound taught her that you surprise yourself by testing your limits; at least that's what she told me. Now it's my chance to test myself, but it's too complicated to start explaining to Mark. Anyway, I know he believes that you have to help women because he's convinced they're the weaker sex. Ha. He exhales, running a hand through his hair, then steps back, defeated. I tuck the hard red rubber-topped crutches under my arms and try again, trying to catch my breath.

It's hard enough walking across the sand on foot, but walking with crutches is like an Olympian test. I continue to slip and slide on the dry mounds of sand. I'm getting it, I say to myself. And then I trip again. "Shit," I yell again. "Shit." Tears flood my eyes. I hear him curse, but he doesn't come to help me. I get back up to my feet.

You're not going to fall again. You can do it.

I make my way, slowly, closing the gap between us, my armpits sore and wet with sweat from the pressure of the crutches, perspiration dripping down my face.

I inch closer and closer to him. He's sitting up in his chair, one arm slung over the back. I approach from behind, inching closer and closer. It feels like I weigh five hundred pounds.

As if he senses me closing in, he turns slightly, takes off his sunglasses, and stares. The barest change of expression crosses his face.

It's enough.

Me hobbling toward him on crutches is so out of the realm of what he expected. He can't hide that, no matter how good he is at keeping his emotions checked. A hint of a smile crosses my face.

I keep going.

The space narrows from yards to feet. He waits, tensed, without taking his eyes off me. In a rush, I'm overcome with happiness that he doesn't come running to help me.

Then it hits me why. He knows better than anyone that I can do it.

It's *because* of him.

When I'm just below the chair, he leaps down so fast I barely see it happen. I stop and the crutches fall away, dropping to the sand. Only now am I suddenly overcome with the drain of energy it took to get me here. Sweat pours down my face. The stinging droplets nearly blind me.

I'm about to topple over into the sand when Pilot reaches out and catches me, drawing me up to him.

"You're crazy," he whispers. "You shouldn't be here. How could they discharge you?"

"They didn't. I left."

"Why didn't you wait for me? I would have come later."

⁓◦⊙◦⁓

I lean my face against his golden shoulder, so warm he may be filled with molten honey. Without warning, tears stream out of my eyes. "Are you some kind of miracle worker? Please, I have to know. That's all I've been thinking about."

"Obviously not," he says, like a painful confession. His face darkens and he looks away. "You got slashed and were close to death."

Is he angry with me or himself? He reads my face.

"I should have *known*," he says, almost pleading.

"Known what?"

"That you were out there. I should have seen it before."

"How could you possibly have known?

He stares out at the water and then back at me. "It's my job to know, Sirena, to be there. It's what I do." He looks away, pained.

"I waited until you walked the other way. You couldn't possibly have seen me."

"You don't understand." He looks into my eyes and sighs. "I see things," he whispers. "I have this...vision. Only

203

this time I didn't. I was blind."

"You saved me. That's all that matters."

"I let it happen, I lost my focus. Only I don't know how. And the stingray. It nearly killed you."

"Stingray?"

He lifts his binoculars suddenly as if he suddenly remembers he's on duty. "You should rest. And I'm working."

"I need to know what happened—please."

"Later."

I glance behind me. Aunt Ellie and Mark are standing by the car, probably watching my every move, trying to read my body language. I'm embarrassed to see them there, my audience.

"I'm coming back, Pilot, when you finish work."

He lifts his head, ignoring that. "I'll carry you back," he says. "Your Aunt is waiting."

"I can walk on my own."

"God, you're stubborn," he says, lifting me up into his arms. "That's part of it."

I start to protest and then stop. "Is that a bad thing?"

"It makes you...difficult, that's all."

⁓⟨◦⟩⁓

I've never been carried by anyone before, at least not since I was an infant. I study Pilot's face to see if it's an

204

effort to support me, but he strides along easily, unfazed by carrying one hundred and twenty five pounds over hot sand like a swami oblivious to burning coals under his feet.

"I don't want to go back," I whisper.

"It shouldn't be much longer."

"After your shift, we'll talk, you promised." I reach for his arm.

"Sirena..."

"Six, right?"

"You have to rest your leg or it'll get worse."

"You won't let it."

He looks at me curiously, but he doesn't say it isn't true.

Ellie and Mark stand by the car like nervous parents. Mark's arms are crossed against his chest, his male body language, just like my dad. The resignation, the private expressions and little quirks that can't hide what's going on isn't *his* idea.

"Stubborn as a goat," Pilot says to Mark, when he reaches the car, but I see his rare smile.

Mark shakes his head.

Pilot helps me into the back seat, sliding his hand above my head as I'm about to bump it on the top of the door. He closes the door gently and waves at Mark. Mark starts the car and pulls out of the parking lot, heading back to the hospital. He's nervous that his cargo is out of its element, like a fresh fish that will start to stink if it's not promptly refrigerated.

They're going to object, but I don't care.

"Let's go back to the house. I can rest with mom and dad. It's just that later I have to see Pilot—when he's finished with his shift."

Mark's shoulders rise and fall and he exhales loudly. In silence, he turns and we head to the house, instead of the hospital. They have to be glad my parents are here now so they can deal with me, even though they haven't seen me in weeks, and they're walking on eggshells when it comes to their only daughter who they're convinced is suicidal.

Only I'm not.

Call it "dis-ease." Not disease. Fear, loneliness, rejection, and isolation all mix in your blood like a toxic cocktail. You take chances. You tempt fate.

What do you have to lose?

It wasn't a death wish, just a test. Only I had no idea what I was up against. No idea.

But the stingray?

My parents are asleep when we get to the house. My dad is stretched out on the downstairs couch and my mom is asleep in my bed. So much for reconciliation.

As usual, Aunt Ellie effortlessly jumps in and takes care of us.

"Maybe lasagna?" she says, sliding a tin foil tray out of the freezer that holds enough for twenty. That's followed by frozen baguettes. Soon she's cutting up a salad. When my parents get up, a feast is on the table.

It's not a stretch to pretend this is a holiday. Only the difference now is that despite everyone's smiley face, we're all slightly traumatized and feel thrown together by circumstances, not by will.

There's an awkward silence as we get seated at the table. We're all dealing with our own private thoughts about how the last seventy-two hours have shaken our lives. Mark jumps in and tries to come to the rescue by talking loudly to my dad about sports and locker room gossip.

"They were the only team ever in the majors with a 12—0 lead and then they blew it," he says. He goes on about someone's rotator cuff injury and how long he'd be out of the game. "That could kill their season," he says, like that would ruin his life.

Mom, Aunt Ellie, and I stare at each other blankly. Like we care? Mom turns and asks Aunt Ellie about the house.

"It's haunted," I say, before Aunt Ellie can open her mouth.

Mom looks at me as though now she's convinced this isn't the daughter who flew to Rhode Island four weeks earlier.

"Haunted?"

"It is, really."

My mom looks at Aunt Ellie, who shrugs and smiles slightly. "Well, yes, but they're friendly ghosts at heart. They wouldn't hurt a fly, right Sirena?"

"I'm living proof." Then I think maybe I'm not such a good example. I'm about to describe the burned out faces, but catch myself. My mom would be out the door, heading to the nearest Motel 6, whether or not they kept the lights on for her.

"Dad knows. Right, Dad?"

He closes his eyes and nods exaggeratedly. He'd never admit it, but I don't think he'd look forward to a stormy night in the attic either.

"But they only come out when there's a storm," I say. "So you're lucky because the weather's supposed to be great for the week."

"Hooray," my mom says.

Aunt Ellie changes the subject and tells us about her books. When she's done and we've all seen the new cover of her newest one, she serves blueberry sorbet. Then I look at my watch. "I told Pilot I'd go back to the beach when his shift ends."

"I'll drive you," Aunt Ellie says, before anyone can say

different. "It's fine."

Maybe everyone is too worn out for a fight, or afraid to start one. For once, my mom and dad look like they're happy to give up their authority. Staying home and doing the dishes looks good to Mark. He wants to avoid another scene.

When we're in the front seat of the car together, I turn to Aunt Ellie. "Thanks."

"Um hmm," she singsongs lightly.

Points for not asking me why or telling me what I'm doing is stupid. She knows I have to.

She parks in the same spot that Mark did and gets the crutches out of the trunk. No wheelchair now. She knows I can go the extra couple of yards without it. She hands me the crutches and stands there, hands on hips.

"When do you want me to come back for you?"

"Pilot will take me home."

"You sure?"

I nod and she gets back in the car.

She sits behind the wheel for a moment and slowly pulls out of the parking lot. I know she's watching me in the rearview mirror. I start the trip across the sand, this time more experienced on the crutches, even though they are rubbing raw the blisters on my underarms. The sun is lower in the sky and I'm tempted to stop and sit in the sand. But I pause and then keep going, the marathon runner who gets a last burst of energy when the finish line is in view.

When I'm almost there I stop and watch as Pilot slides his tank top over his head. He grabs a white T-shirt and is about to pull it on when he turns and sees me. He stands there, frozen, his eyes widening.

I feel like I'm watching him strip and I can't breathe.

He catches himself and pulls his shirt on quickly, throwing a towel around his neck. He lifts his backpack and walks toward me as I wait.

"I'll take you back," he says, matter-of-factly.

"We have to talk."

He exhales and shakes his head. "Okay...I have the Jeep."

He hoists me over his shoulder like he's bringing home the catch of the day, and he heads for the parking lot. I can't imagine what we look like, me holding the crutches out as if I'm bearing a divining rod.

I climb into the car and put on the seat belt. It closes with a loud click. He turns on the car and glances out his rearview mirror as he backs up and pulls out of the lot. I have no idea where we're going. It doesn't matter.

"There's water in the cooler," he says, pointing to an insulated bag at my feet.

I shake my head.

A few miles down the road, he pulls off the main road and heads down a narrow, unpaved path surrounded by tall beach grass.

"You'll like this beach," he says. "Very few people know about it."

He goes to the back and takes out a blanket, then comes around to my side of the car and helps me out. "I can walk on my own, really."

"It's better if you don't. Not yet. " He carries me out to a beach with no one on it. The water is calm and the tide is low. I'm sorry that we can't walk for miles together.

The beach is a sandy paradise that's completely private and empty for us to share. It feels like he's given me a gift. My own beach.

And then the anxious me rears her head. Does he bring other girls here? Is this where they hang out? I try to push those thoughts out of my head.

Pilot puts me down gently and shakes out the blanket. I sit down and he drops down next to me, propping himself up on his elbows. He stares at my leg where the gash was and then out at the water.

"What do you want to know?" he asks directly. He does not want to have this conversation.

"I want to know what you did. How you did it. They were going to amputate my leg and then miraculously, it got better."

"It did," he says, eyes wide.

I smirk and he smiles.

"You have to tell me. I have to know."

"I learned things from my family, from my father and my grandfather," he says, smoothing the sand between us.

"Your grandfather?"

"Tonio."

"Who?"

"You *know* him," he insists. "The painter."

"Antonio...*He's* your grandfather?"

"You honestly didn't know?"

"He never told me anything." I think of all the things I said to him about Pilot. Things I never would have admitted if I had known they were related. He knew I liked Pilot—enough to steal his painting of him—but he never mentioned that Pilot was his grandson to spare me the embarrassment. So now it's clear why he was able to paint him more than once and how he knew his face so well that the picture almost spoke. They were flesh and blood.

Pilot shakes his head. "He never talks about himself," he says, as though he knows what I'm thinking. "He never tells people what anyone tells him. He's protective."

"I love him." I'm surprised by what I blurted out and more than that, that I'm telling his grandson.

"*Everyone* loves him." He grins. "Especially women. No matter how old or young."

"So what did he teach you?"

He narrows his eyes and looks at me curiously.

I feel my cheeks burn. "I mean about healing."

He stares out at the water again. "It's not so much *what* he taught me. It's what he helped me discover... about myself...my family..." He hesitates. "Some people just have natural gifts, and our family...we have a kind of vision when it comes to seeing who needs help and drawing on powers inside us. It's not something I can put into words. I don't even understand it myself. I just know that sometimes...not always...I can help people heal."

"Cody, too?"

"Cody, too."

"I didn't realize it at first, but after Cody got better when no one thought he would, and then the man on the beach started breathing again, I knew it was something you did."

He stares ahead of him, lost in his thoughts.

"How did you know you could help me?"

He shakes his head and keeps staring. "I don't always know and it's so frustrating. Sometimes it doesn't work. Or sometimes it doesn't work as well as it should...I...I just don't know all the time."

"Yes, you do."

He turns and looks at me challengingly. "How do you know that?"

"I can't heal, but I can read your face." I run my hand from the top of his forehead down over the side of his face like a blind person trying to understand what someone looks like. "And I know that you don't give up." A tiny muscle at the side of his jaw starts to quiver like a fine barometer, responding to the slightest change in the atmosphere.

"I want to know you. I want to know how you do it. You saved my life." My face is so close I'm nearly kissing him.

"It's something inside…I go outside myself to get help from the spirits." He watches me to see how I react to his words. "You can't put everything into words and make it knowable, Sirena…It's a connection."

"Antonio says when people get sick it's because they lose their spirit."

"That's what he taught me," he says. "Part of the soul escapes—the way people shut down to get away from pain or loss. Only sometimes part of the soul doesn't come back. A healer works to make the person whole again."

"And with me?"

"Your soul left your body," he says. "You were almost dead."

He turns to me and our lips accidentally touch. Instead of pulling back, I lean toward him, pressing my mouth against his. He kisses me back this time, his mouth deliciously sweet and salty. We seem molded to fit together. I fall back on the blanket and he comes with me, as eager for me as I am for him. Seconds go by and then something snaps. He sits up, abruptly.

"It's harder to protect you if I'm close to you, Sirena." His voice is hoarse and imploring. "That blinds me. I can't let that happen again."

"You have no choice."

⁓❦⁓

He drops down next to me, his arm resting over his forehead. I move toward him, leaning my head on his chest. His heartbeat is strong and rhythmic. I reach up and trace my finger along the side of his jaw. "I never met someone who performs miracles."

"I just try to help people heal when things go wrong. It's different. It has to do with infusing a spirit…"

"You said you hear my heartbeat—at least I think you did."

"I can."

"That scares me."

"You wanted to know."

"I've never heard anything like that before. Is it just me?"

"It's with some people—people who I set my mind on knowing. I know it sounds strange. Abnormal. But it's something I can pick up. When I heard you panicking, I swam out to get you." He shakes his head. "But it was too late."

I lean up on one hand and look at him, but he's lost in

his own thoughts, his face impassive, resolute.

"Why do you think you failed? I'm here, I'm still alive."

"But you were in such pain, do you remember? "You lost so much blood. I swam out there too late. I didn't see the stingray." He bites at the corner of his lip. "It shouldn't have even been there. Then after I pulled you out, you were almost dead." He shakes his head. "Then the infection, what was going to happen to you. I couldn't stand it. If I hadn't pulled the power…"

"The power?"

"The power. The blackout."

I sit up and stare at him. "I thought it was storm. The whole town lost power, they said."

"The hospital has a generator. The hospital never blacks out. There was no other way for me to get you out of there. They were about to cut off your leg. I had no choice, so I turned it off."

I stare at him and shake my head. "But what if someone had died? What if there was an operation going on?"

"There wasn't. It's a small hospital," he says, reading my confusion. "What?"

"I sensed something…only I didn't know quite what it was."

"What *what* was?"

"I had this feeling of calm, of peace, even though my

leg was killing me and I was burning up."

"It was my nearness. That was part of it. I had to help you calm down or I couldn't have focused. If you were in a panic, I wouldn't have been able to connect with you...to heal you"

"But you did. That's what matters."

He turns away, staring out at the water, absentmindedly running his hand back and forth along the sand between us. I study his fingers, the shape of his hands.

Did I just see what I think I did? I lean closer. How is that possible? Tiny granules of sand rise up to his fingers as if he's a lightning rod that draws the power of the earth to him.

He turns from the water and sees me watching. Quickly, he pulls his hand back.

"Did you just...?"

"Sshh," he says.

He gets up and crouches over me. "Lie back," he says. "Close your eyes." He presses his hands on either side of my head. Immediately a flow of warmth spreads over me.

"This is how I do it," he murmurs. "This is how I heal."

I think he's poured his heart into mine.

thirty-one

W̲e have to get back," he whispers. He brushes a strand of hair away from my face.

"What time is it?"

"Almost nine."

It's dark out. When did that happen? I rub my eyes, inhaling the scent of him on my skin. "I don't want to go."

"They'll be worried," he says, getting to his feet. The look on his face says it's settled in his mind. It's useless to argue. He reaches his hands out and pulls me to my feet.

"Let me try to walk." I start to hobble on one foot.

"The wound was deep. It's not healed up inside." He lifts me and carries me back to the car. I press my head against his shoulder to hide my smile.

His car is the only one in the lot. We climb in and drive off, leaving our secret hideaway. We ride back in silence, connected now. There's no reason to speak.

I can only imagine what Ellie and Mark and my parents

are thinking. Knowing my dad, he's combing the beach now for my body. I'd never tell Pilot what he's like. If I did, he'd never take me anywhere again. When he pulls up to the house, my dad is standing guard on the porch, but he's on his best behavior, I can tell. My mom probably shouted out a warning before she let him go out.

"Missed dinner," he says, flatly. He looks at us coolly.

"I'm sorry, Dad. I'll eat the leftovers, okay?"

His face is visibly relieved, though. I'm back and alive.

"I'm sorry, sir," Pilot says. "I hope we didn't worry you. It was a beautiful night so we were on the beach."

He leaves it at that. Points for honesty.

My dad nods. He's not about to lecture the lifeguard who saved the life of his only child.

As I walk into the house, I sense something is different. I feel renewed in some way. But how?

⁓⊙⌒

It only occurs to me after Pilot waves from the car and pulls out. And then it's so clear. He didn't help me out of the car this last time. He didn't even walk around to help me. At the absolutely same moment I think of that, my dad stares at me as if he's seen a ghost.

I'm walking perfectly on my own.

"Jesus, Mary, and Joseph," he whispers, under his breath.

219

thirty-two

Aunt Ellie drives my parents to the airport. They're caught in the middle ground. They don't want to stay or leave, and the hardest decision is what to do with me. Drag me back with them, going against my wishes? Or let me stay with the risk of something else happening that they could have prevented?

Aunt Ellie has the final say in convincing them to let me finish the summer with her. She trusts me, in spite of everything. On top of that, it's hard to argue for going back to swampy Houston in August when the temperatures hit a hundred, and a machete couldn't cut through the humidity.

So the beach wins out. And so do I.

My dad rarely shows emotion, but I swear that tears well up in his eyes when he kisses me good-bye at the airport. "Allergies," he comes up with, out of nowhere. "Take care of yourself," he says. "No stupid stuff, okay?"

Stupid stuff? Does that mean going swimming when there are riptides, following lifeguards to deserted beaches, or all of the above? Not sure, exactly, but to make it easier for my dad, I don't ask for clarification.

"Promise." He needs to hear that.

"Be careful," is all my mom says. The umbrella advice. "Take care of yourself."

"I'll be fine. Don't worry, please."

My mom holds out her hands. "Me not worry? It's in the genes," she says, studying me as if it's for the last time.

Aunt Ellie and I wait at the gate until they both disappear down the jetway to the plane.

"That was easy," she says, as we head to the car.

⁓◦⊙◦⁓

When I hear her voice on the phone it throws me. "Marissa?"

She starts to laugh. "Did you forget already?"

"Omigod, how did you get to use the phone?" In a rush, I realize how much I've missed her.

"I made up a story, at least I think it's a story. I told them my best friend nearly drowned."

There's silence on the line.

"Oh God, you did," she says, her voice dropping. "Are you okay now? You're scaring me to death, Sirena."

"I'm okay, I am," I say, my voice cracking. "But... there's so much to tell you. "It was just...so scary. I got pulled out by a riptide..." I leave it at that.

"I knew something was wrong. I knew it. It was the first time that you didn't write. And you sounded so down." She pauses. "What happened?

"The water was rough and it pulled me out."

"Why did you go in? I mean, don't they keep everybody out when they know it's dangerous?"

"I thought I'd just cool off...It was hot."

"He was the one who saved you?"

"He heard me calling for help."

"You were testing him," she says.

"What?"

"You were making him prove himself to you."

"It was the *riptide*, Marissa..."

"I know you, Sirena."

"I didn't mean for anything to happen," I whisper. "I had no idea..."

"It's over," she says. "Thank God you're safe."

❧

Aunt Ellie has a library with a wall of science books. I get on a ladder and reach to the top for a book about sea life. I turn to the index: *Stingrays*.

"Stingrays are most often found in shallow coastal

waters of temperate seas," it says. No mention of Rhode Island. It goes on to talk about the types of stingrays and how they're shy and nonaggressive, unless they're threatened—in my case, pounced on. Reflexively, they lash out with their serrated tails, causing a jagged laceration from the teeth of the spine. To make it worse, the underside of the tail injects a venom that immediately causes excruciating pain and can be fatal to humans.

Now I understand.

The unimaginable pain, the paralysis. That was the last thing I remember as I sank to the bottom.

"Unlike most other fish toxins," the book goes on, "the venom of stingrays can be broken down with high heat." The wound should be immersed in very hot, but not scalding water for up to ninety minutes, it says. Any bits of the bony spine should be removed.

I think of Pilot and how his hands sent deep, penetrating heat surging through me. Not only did he pull me out of the water; he detoxed me. I close the book and put it back up on the shelf. The pieces of the mystery are coming together, only one question remains. There aren't any stingrays in Rhode Island.

So how did that one get there?

⁓

I take a bath before I go to bed, drying myself and then

smoothing lavender scented cream over my legs. The marks where they took out the stitches are barely visible. The pink, jagged scar is so faint it's hard to see anymore. I put more cream on the hurt leg, caressing it with my hand because it ties me to Pilot. I need to see him again, to learn more about him.

But before I do, I want to go to the beach and find Antonio. I'm convinced that he played a role in saving me, but I can't help wondering why he didn't come see me in the hospital. He's old and it's probably hard for him to get around, but I thought he'd visit. I thought he'd be there. I haven't seen him in almost two weeks.

Even though I'm still a little stiff, I put on my helmet and take the bike. It's more of an effort than I expected, but I keep going, determined to build myself up again. When I manage to get to the spot where Antonio usually sits, I see his chair is there as usual and he's in it. The umbrella is opened up next to him, but under it is someone else—someone I'm stunned to recognize. The hair first. Then the body. And when she turns toward me, her face.

The blonde.

I know it's stupid, but the first thing I feel is jealousy. I've been replaced. I get ready to start pedaling away. He has other company, he doesn't need me around. I'm crazy, I know, but I can't help it. He's eighty years old. Still, I wonder if she's drawn to Antonio the way I am. Before I can turn, Antonio senses me there and waves.

"Sirena," he calls. "Come, sit with us."

I stare back and stand still, caught. Not knowing what else to do, I drop my bike on its side and take off my helmet.

<hr/>

I try to hide that I'm disappointed to share him. I can't be as open as I usually am. I sit down next to Edna and stroke her back, casually ignoring the girl.

"You look wonderful," Antonio says. "The color, it's back in your cheeks."

Did he see me when it wasn't? I can't ask if he visited me in the hospital, or if he didn't, why not, so I just smile and shrug. "I'm so much better. It doesn't even hurt anymore."

"Bravo," he says. He gestures for me to sit on the blanket next to him. "Do you know Adriana?"

I shake my head.

"You've never met?" Why is he so surprised?

"Pilot told me about you," she says. "I'm glad you're better."

I narrow my eyes. *Does she really mean it?* "Thanks," I say softly.

I look over at Antonio and see something I've never seen before. A purple bruise in the crease of his arm.

"What happened to you?" He's never been sick, he said. There's never anything wrong with him, so what is that?

"Ah, that, it's nothing." He waves his hand in the air, dismissively.

"That's where he gave blood," Adriana says, like a little child who can't keep a secret. "Why don't you tell her?"

"Tell me what?"

"He gave his blood to you," Adriana says. "So did Pilot. More than he should have. I don't think it was safe. Why didn't you tell her?"

"Is that true?"

Antonio nods. "You lost so much, *querida*. We wanted to help." He shakes his head. "We did what we could."

"That was so good of you, so kind. How come no one told me?" The tears start to blur my sight.

"Don't cry," Antonio insists. "Please, Sirena, you'll make me sad. It's over now. Be happy. Now we are like one." He reaches for my hand and holds it firmly in his. His hand is twice the size of mine. "And the gift that I left for you in the hospital—did you get it?"

"Gift? No. I...I didn't even know you were there."

"Go back and ask about it at the desk," he says. "I left it with the nurse. They're still holding it for you, I'm sure."

I know I shouldn't ask, only I can't help it. "What is it?"

"Something special...You will see."

I don't look forward to going back there. I've alienated half the staff, I think, by going AWOL. Aunt Ellie got calls from the hospital looking for me. They were annoyed that I left without checking with the doctors and getting discharge papers. But Aunt Ellie and Mark smoothed it over.

Still, how could I resist picking up a gift from Antonio?

"Sirena," one of the nurses on the floor calls out to me. I wait for her to lecture me, but instead she watches me walk and shakes her head. "You're our best advertising."

"Well..." I leave it at that.

"Antonio said he dropped off a package for me... before I left, I guess."

"Let me look." She pokes through the drawers beneath her desk and finally comes up with a box of candy. "This?"

Candy? I feel a sinking disappointment. "I don't know," I say, taking the box from her. I turn it over and finally make out someone else's name scrawled on the bottom. "No, that's not it..."

"Oh," she says, still searching.

Just when I think she's going to say she doesn't have anything, she slides a narrow cylinder covered in navy blue silk out of a cabinet. There's a dark blue ribbon around it that holds a note card. What could possibly fit inside, a pair of chopsticks? Another figa?

I take it from her and go outside into the sunlight. I don't want anyone else to be around when I open it.

Whatever it is, I know it will be special. And different. I sit on a bench and two girls walk by. As soon as they pass, I open the small envelope, working hard not to tear it.

"To Sirena, fine artist and my treasured friend: My vision and a part of my soul—now in your hands."

I open the tube and turn it upside down. A narrow, red silk bag slides out. I open the flap and take out a paintbrush. Sable bristles and an intricately carved ivory handle, slightly yellowed with age. I imagine wearing it on a silk cord around my neck, like a piece of jewelry.

Only this isn't a piece of jewelry, even though it could be. I've seen this brush in Antonio's hand so often that I think of it as a part of him. I close my hand over it and remember how he used it. Now it's mine and I can't imagine living up to it. I slide it back into its red silk bag and put it into the tube, slipping it into an inside pocket of my bag.

I have to go thank him—now—but before I go to see Antonio, I want to sit by myself and think about his gift and what it means. How could he have given me something like this? It's such a special brush, a part of him, like a writer's favorite pen, or a magical talisman that an artist keeps nearby for inspiration. This isn't just a gift. He's sharing a part of himself with me.

I turn my bike around and take a path parallel to the water. The sky is blindingly blue and there's a light breeze. I stare down at my legs pumping effortlessly now as if nothing had ever happened and the accident was a dark dream. I look around at cars going by and people walking. None of them would believe what has happened to me.

⁓⊙⊱⊰⊙⁓

I'm not sure of how to get to the beach. I wasn't paying much attention to the road when he drove. I didn't know where we were going and it didn't matter anyway. He could have headed to California and I would have said it was fine.

I remember a right turn, I think, but which one? Does Antonio know about the beach? He might even go there sometimes to paint. I think of his picture of the sky. That beach, that expanse of sand and water with no one on it, might have been his inspiration.

There are several streets that lead to the water. Which did we take? I wish I didn't get so lost in my thoughts and in my daydreams. I should learn to pay attention, to watch out. I make the first turn I see, but it ends at a private road ending at a gray shingled house on the water. There's a sign on the closed gate. "No trespassing."

I head back to the bike path and keep going until I come to another road. Only this one stops before the water. Wrong again. I stop, wipe the sweat off my foreheads and try to get my bearings.

After another quarter mile or so and there's another turn-off. That must be it. There are no cars along the road.

229

I ride along the sandy path feeling the wind picking up, mounds of blown sand beneath the tires loosening their grip. I cross a bumpy patch and then up ahead, and the ocean appears. I drop my bike in the sand when I get to a fence. "Parking with beach stickers only," a small, white-weathered sign says. I make my way along the narrow path with tall, celery-colored sea grass on either side of me, swaying in the wind.

A strange sensation takes over me as I walk closer and closer.

I'm entering Pilot's private world.

Trespassing.

thirty-three

I walk to the end of the path and there it is before me: the magical stretch of pristine beach.

How do I know?

Not the way the dunes slope gently to the sea. Not the house with the porthole windows, like a stationary ocean liner blown off course. Or the home nearby with the balcony and the pale green rocking chairs, so close to the water that it could all be swallowed by a giant wave. And not the abandoned blue pail and shovel, still poking out of the sand almost a week later, like markers of a toddler's turf.

It's him, out there before me.

The tall, rangy physique. The straw-colored hair grazing his golden shoulders, board shorts clinging to his lean hips.

Only he has company.

Adriana.

They're not sitting on his blanket watching the waves, the way we did. And they're not talking. They're knee deep in the surf, his arm loosely around her waist. She leans against him, her platinum hair covering her shoulders like fine-spun gold. They're a fairytale snapshot of serenity and unimaginable beauty, facing the sea. They were born to be together, the fairy tale prince and princess.

As slowly as I arrived, I retreat, stepping back, catlike, as if despite the blowing wind, the waves lapping against the shore, and their total absorption in each other, they still might be able to make out my footsteps, the stray cat who has come upon their private oasis.

I pedal as fast as I can to get as far from this beach as quickly as is humanly possible. What was I thinking? Why did I want to come here, of all places? It's his beach, I don't belong here. I don't belong anywhere near him ever again. Did I think I was the only one in his life? He's the most perfect looking male in the universe, so that's a totally absurd thought. I feel sickened, betrayed.

I head back to the safety of Antonio's beach. He might still be there; it's only seven. So what if he's Pilot's grandfather? I need his comforting presence. I need to lean on him, be sheltered by him. He takes me in, all-knowing, protective, accepting, no matter what.

Only he isn't there.

He must have packed up early or had something else to do. He meets friends for dinner sometimes at a little restaurant at the end of the beach. I may go riding past to see if I can spot him there.

I know so little about Antonio. Where does he live when he's not outside painting? Where does he go off season? So many people come for the summer and then vanish for months at a time.

⁂

Aunt Ellie gives me a strange look when I get home. "Are you okay, Sirena?"

"Why shouldn't I be?"

"I don't know you just seem...pale."

Aunt Ellie's upset, I can tell. I want to ask her if she's ever had her heart torn apart. Or what you do when you feel betrayed by someone and hurt so badly that you feel you can't live in your skin and you'll go out of your mind? I want to ask her if she's ever cared about somebody with every cell in her body and if there's any way you can make the stabbing ache go away when you find out they're in love with someone else.

But why? Nothing she or anyone else could say would make a difference. I force myself to sound normal.

"I was looking for Antonio. He gave me a paintbrush

233

as a gift." I take it out of my bag and hold it out to her. She examines it carefully. "He left it at the hospital for me but I didn't find out about it until today."

"It's beautiful," she says. "It looks so old." She smiles. "It goes with the easel."

"Was that his?"

She nods. "I told him you were coming and he offered it."

"I always had a feeling about it…about the person who owned it before me…Now I know where those thoughts came from." I shake my head. "Anyway, I wanted to thank him, but by the time I got the beach, he wasn't there anymore."

"There's a birthday party for his gallery owner tonight," she says. "Just a small party, but he's hosting it. I saw him leaving the beach early to get ready."

<hr/>

Mark comes over for dinner and we eat grilled scallops, baked potatoes, and salad. He works hard at making conversation with me, undeterred by my one-word answers. He reminds me of a stand-up comic who keeps on with the one-liners, even when he knows the audience isn't with him. When we finally finish and Aunt Ellie gets up to clear the table, Mark opens the back door.

"Want to get some air?" he says.

I shrug and follow him outside. There are two wooden

chairs on the patio and we sit facing each other. He sips a glass of red wine and stares at me, smiling over the rim.

"What is it, Sirena?"

"What do you mean?"

"I know you by now," he says, in his warm, gravelly voice. I look out at the water and then back at him. He fixes me with his warm, brown eyes and waits.

"People hurt you sometime, you know?"

"Yeah," he nods, looking off, shaking his head slightly. He turns back to me and holds my gaze, waiting.

"I mean, maybe they don't mean to, they don't do it intentionally, but that's how it feels."

He grins. "I used to feel like I was a punching bag. I got beaten up by life all the time."

"That's how I feel."

He puts the glass on the arm of the chair and leans toward me. "Who hurt you, Sirena?"

I shake my head, my eyes full of tears. I shouldn't tell him, I know, but I have to tell someone. "Pilot."

He leans his head to the side, narrowing his eyes. "How?"

"He's got a girlfriend, Mark, and I can't stand it. I thought he liked me, but then I saw them together. They didn't know I was there. Do you know how much that hurts?"

"Oh, baby," he says. He's silent as he looks at the

ground, thinking about what to say. "Did he tell you he doesn't want to see you anymore?"

"Not really."

"Then screw the girlfriend."

I want to laugh but start crying instead.

"If he lets a beautiful babe like you get away, then he's out of his gourd."

He hands me a tissue and I blow my nose. "You think so?"

"Any sane guy would fall at your feet," he says. "Don't forget that."

"Mark?"

"What?"

"Do you miss your wife?"

His face changes. "Sure, I do," he says. "Sure. But you take the punches, and you go on. You can't stand still, Sirena. And you can't feel sorry for yourself, there's just no point to it, you know? There's a lot of good stuff out there and you have to move on, you have to find it. Life's one big treasure hunt."

The screen door opens and Aunt Ellie pokes her head out. "Are you guys ever coming in for dessert?"

"What are we having?" I ask.

"Lobster ice cream," Mark says.

"Are you kidding?" I'm not crying anymore.

"Had you going."

After dinner I go upstairs and take out paper and paints. I open the navy blue cylinder and turn it upside down. Antonio's brush slides out of its hiding place. I'll do a quick still life of my bed and the table next to it with the inky blue bowl of chalk-white seashells. I work quickly with the brush, each stroke clear and sure. My hand is expert with the paint. The brush glides smoothly over the paper as if it's in tune with an internal rhythm. As if the brush is painting by itself.

For the first time in as long as I can remember, everything in my head is traveling through my hand and coming out on the paper. Twelve o'clock, one, then two. I stay up longer than I expected, working with an intensity and purpose. At close to three in the morning I stop. I drop on the bed without washing up.

The dreams start as soon as I close my eyes. There's a dark curtain rising on another universe, some vast, unknown space like a strange, unexplored planet where no human has ever gone before. Antonio is there looking at me. His mahogany eyes are darker and more penetrating than I have ever seen them.

"Sirena," he intones, in his deep, full voice, like an off-stage narrator. He's watching me, seeing me paint. Everything that I painted swirls around me, all the colors of the universe bleeding onto a giant canvas. But it is Antonio's presence, his soul that fills the stage. He's touching my hands, holding them. His skin is warm like Pilot's, overheated. It's a healing warmth, an energy. A golden, beneficent heat spreads over me as he infuses me with his strength and power. I see a vision of him holding the paintbrush, his fingerprints pressing it, leaving behind his DNA, his genetic prowess. He's transferred all that to me along with the paintbrush.

Our creative link.

It's the same feeling I got when Aunt Ellie gave me the easel, only more so. I'm the direct recipient of Antonio's talents, his gifts, his vision, his worldliness, his confidence.

It's my destiny to paint, to create. The world around us is a giant canvas, and the sky is a palette smeared with swirls of every vivid color—magenta, citron, lavender, and acid green for me to play and experiment with. There's a magnetic field around me and everything buzzes with electrified life, clarity and possibility. Every color is in its freshest, purest form. The bluest blue I have ever seen. The duskiest pinks, the most orange-red coral. Deep stormy grays and charcoal blacks. My senses have been flooded with the spectrum and the possibilities of where to put the colors. My hands are the instruments and I'm a giant puppet who will paint and keep painting until I'm too tired to hold the brush anymore. My eyelids flutter, my breathing is so intense that my heart quivers nervously in my chest like a captive butterfly. I wake up with a start—soaked with sweat. I sit up in bed and a flood of tears come.

I know what happened. I understand the dream.

Only I'm powerless to change it.

thirty-four

Pilot comes to the house to tell me. Aunt Ellie couldn't bear to. He's wearing a pressed white shirt and dark pants. He stands as tall and straight as a sailboard mast. He doesn't have to utter a word. My heart sinks.

Antonio.

"God, Pilot...What will we do without him?"

He shakes his head and touches my shoulders, gently pulling me toward him. He stares hard out the window, afraid to speak, I think. He takes in a deep breath and waits.

"After the service we'll spread his ashes over the water," he says, haltingly. "He loved that beach more than any other place in the world so he'll always be there, a part of it from now on. We'll see him in the ocean. We'll feel him there with us forever. We won't lose him...We can't."

His words hang in the air between us.

My heart will break at the service. I can't face it. But; go? I have to. My mind anchors me by stubbornly fixating on the smallest abstract details—the way the water darkens as the clouds shift, the slant of the sun, the soft feel of the sand shifting under my feet. Things in nature that change, but never leave.

The clouds are low in the sky. In the distance there's a rumbling of thunder. A storm is moving in. The end of the summer is closing in. Hurricane season is here and everything will change in the weeks to come.

For me it already has.

—⁓☙⁓—

A big crowd gathers on the beach for the funeral. A dark gray cloud of mourners huddle together. There are so many faces I've never seen before. Aunt Ellie and I stand together, to the side. Antonio touched so many people in a personal way. He opened his heart to everyone he met, welcoming every new person and experience. At the very least, people knew him through his paintings, if not his reputation.

Adriana stands close to Pilot, her head held high. She's wearing a dark, flowing dress. Sunglasses shield her eyes. No outward attempt to look glamorous, only she can't help it, her mane of golden hair blowing in the breeze over her tanned, lean shoulders. She has the aura of a celebrity,

241

a regal bearing. Antonio probably had lots of special friends our age. I flash back to the sting of seeing her on the beach together with Pilot, so close they were almost breathing with one breath.

A local priest, a friend of Antonio, leads the service. Edna is crouched at his side, her head down, her moist eyes fixed on the distance as if she's wondering what she's going to do for the rest of her life without him, her life's companion. There's something so stoic about her bearing that I stifle a deep cry in my throat.

I stare out at the beach while I listen, numb with stabbing sadness, imagining him sitting there looking out, the delicate paintbrush in his oversized brown hand, his easel in front of him with swirls of brilliant colors, the brown cardboard box of chocolate chip cookies for energy and sweetness. His props are displayed there now. The thermos of water and lemon. A book of poems nearby for when he stopped painting and wanted inspiration from the written world. He was always so attentive to others. He'd be narrowing his eyes, listening while he painted. Pilot laughed one day and said, "Antonio can't concentrate without a paintbrush in his hand."

If Antonio were here right now he'd wave aside all the praise and shrug his broad, heavy shoulders. He'd throw back his head of dark, thick hair and laugh his deep, throaty laugh because everyone was making such a ceremony of a man who died in his sleep as peacefully as he lived, during his early evening nap, Edna resting next to him, her snoring like soothing white noise.

"Beloved?" he'd scoff. "I was a man, that's all. A painter. Sometimes good, sometimes not." I remember him holding his hands out to the side. "When it works, it's wonderful," he said. "And when it doesn't…" He gestured helplessly, not finishing the sentence. He was accepting, able to handle what came his way.

Did it take eighty years to become that way? Or was he just lucky?

The temperature is dropping, the air growing thinner and cooler. I didn't think to bring a sweater. I'm always shivering but now, to my surprise, even though I'm wearing a sleeveless dress, I'm not cold.

Aunt Ellie and I stroll back to the house together after the service. "Such a touching remembrance," she says, her voice trailing off.

I nod, afraid to speak.

"It's so sad for Pilot and Adriana, too. He was their only family."

I stop and turn to her. "*Their* only family?"

"Antonio took care of both of them. Pilot's father died when he was small. I don't know what happened to his mother. No one talks about her.

"And Adriana? She's always with them." I can't keep the annoyance out of my voice. "Pilot must be so in love with her."

"It's not like that," Aunt Ellie says.

"What do you mean?"

"Antonio spent a long time with her mother. I'm kind of fuzzy on all this—I never felt it was my business to ask—but I think her mother was Antonio's girlfriend after his wife died. Adriana was almost like a daughter."

"I always see her with Pilot. It's obvious that he's so close to her."

"I don't know how it is between them," Aunt Ellie says. "I guess you have to ask him."

Is it possible that I read it all wrong? I think about all my jealous feelings toward her. How I resent her. Could it be that she's just... what...maybe like a sister to him? I have to ask him. I have to find out for sure. Only not yet. It's the wrong time.

But just the fact that I might have been wrong...changes everything.

thirty-five

Somewhere outside of my web of sleep I sense a faint rumbling. I open my eyes and turn toward the clock. Red digital numbers glow in the blackness: two AM. The sounds grow loud, coming closer, barreling through the wide silence of the night like an oncoming train. The roaring builds:

One minute.

Two minutes.

Three minutes—then mysteriously stops.

Dead silence.

I sit up in bed, then walk toward the window. A single street lamp casts a gilded shadow on the dark street and there in the center of the pool of light is a motorcycle. The driver sits, legs spread wide, straddling it. Blond hair reaching his shoulders.

Pilot.

He sits completely still, like a messenger from some other galaxy carrying a secret I'm destined to intuit.

No helmet, so unlike him. I run downstairs, but just before I get there, he guns the engine and quickly takes off as if he abruptly changed his mind.

"Pilot! Pilot!" I call into the blackness, as my heart pounds faster and harder. There's no way he could hear me, but I call him again and again, overcome with desperation. Then a window creaks opens in the house.

"Sirena, are you okay?"

Damn. Aunt Ellie. "Yes, yes, I'm fine," I call back. She accepts that. I can't imagine why.

I creep to the edge of the lawn, out of the view from her window, and wait, hugging my knees like a six-year-old. I don't know what's happening or what it means, but my body has registered high alert and my heart won't stop slamming in my chest.

For no reason, I whisper his name, so softly it's almost like praying.

"Pilot, Pilot."

In the distance, the sound of his bike gets lower and lower until there's nothing at all but a vast, encompassing silence. Still disoriented from being wrenched awake, I lean back in the grass and doze off, losing track of time. Finally, I get to my feet and head back to the house. I ease open the screen door to try to muffle its rusty whine. As it's about to slam closed behind me, the rumbling begins to build again. I catch my breath and stand completely still. Very gently I ease the door back open and step outside, catching it before it slams behind me. Aunt Ellie has gone back to sleep, I'm sure.

I walk out to the road and wait in the darkness like a solitary hitchhiker.

One minute.

Two minutes.

Three minutes.

Four minutes.

The roar grows in intensity. I step back as the blinding beam of the headlight flashes on and off me as it follows the curves of the road and finally hits me directly. I raise my hand to shield my eyes as Pilot slows the bike and stops inches in front of me. The engine goes silent.

His hair is wild and windblown, his eyes red and rimmed with sadness. The stoic, repressed tower of strength has been replaced with a grief-stricken Pilot who looks as though life has turned on him.

There are no words to say. Nothing spoken that will change things, but his need for closeness is almost palpable. If only, if only. I don't let myself think what might be, I only think of what is right now. I climb mutely behind him on the bike as if it's my rightful place and cling to him, my legs pressed against his, two bodies joined as one. I think of being behind him on the surfboard. This time it's less clear who's saving whom.

He steers the bike out to the road again and picks up speed, the power of flying down an empty road like a hallucinogenic drug. I rub my cheek back and forth against the softness of his shirt, over the hard muscles of his back and he leans into me.

I have no idea where we're going—somewhere, anywhere, nowhere—it doesn't matter.

He slows finally at a beach and we park. The water is strangely still. Pilot puts an arm around my waist and pulls me close to him. We walk one mile, then another as a stream of tears runs down his perfect face.

We stop at the water's edge and he stares out, lost in thought. I want to say something, anything, to try to make him feel better. "You lost the closest person in the world... He was a miraculous man."

Pilot looks at me directly and nods his head. He drops to the sand, pulling me down next to him. "He was exactly that," he says. "Do you know what a shaman is?"

"Antonio told me, he told me about his father."

"Well *he* was one too," Pilot says, "even though he would never really admit it."

We sit in silence. Pilot raises his head. It's almost as though he's listening to Antonio in his head.

"What?" I ask for no reason. "What are you thinking?"

"About how he saved people," he says.

"Who did he save?"

He shrugs, running a hand through his hair.

"Tell me, please."

"People here who were sick...and once..."

"What?"

He looks at me directly. "A girl on the beach," he says, almost like a confession. "She was drowning. He swam out and saved her."

"And?" I don't know why, but I know there's more. I look at his face and see something about it that pains him. "Where were you?"

He shakes his head back and forth slowly.

"It's something I never told anyone," he says. "It happened a long time ago. You asked me a while ago if I had ever *not* saved someone..." He bites the corner of his lip. "I didn't tell you the truth...There was this girl...three years ago." He stops again, reliving it. "She was...obsessed with me in some kind of sick way."

"What happened?"

"She was crazy...I don't know. She tried to get me to like her, to pay attention to her..."

I hold my breath, a knot in my gut.

"She swam out too far one day and pretended she was drowning. I pulled her out even though I knew it was a ploy."

"So?"

"I didn't say anything, but then just a few days later she did it a second time. I told her I knew she was faking it. I said if it happened again, I would ignore her. I told her she was putting other people's lives at risk."

I wait for him to go on.

"Except she did it one last time. Only this time I think she really was trying to kill herself. She did it just as I was walking off the beach at the end of my shift."

He stands there, staring out at the water, as if he's frozen.

"What happened, Pilot?"

"I heard her scream, Sirena. I was back at the parking lot. Too far to hear her, but I did. I heard her and I *ignored* it. I thought she was faking, I didn't think she needed help. I didn't want to play that game. Only I was wrong."

"Did she drown?"

"She would have, but Tonio saved her. He was leaving the beach too and he heard her. He heard the voice in his head and he ran back and swam out to her. She was far out by then, way beyond where the waves broke. She never would have made it back, and I can't ever forget what I did and what could have happened. If it wasn't for Tonio..."

I reach out and take his hand. I can't stand the suffering in his face.

"I didn't do my job, Sirena...and then when you

almost drowned—"

"You came as soon as you heard me…"

"But I couldn't get there in time and you were in such terrible shape—I began to relive something I had tried to put out of my mind, something that haunted me. I thought it was some kind of divine punishment. And now there's no Tonio anymore," Pilot says, "no one to intervene. No one with that higher consciousness, or whatever you want to call it."

"You can't think that way. You have to make peace with yourself and go on."

"I know," Pilot says.

"And he left us so much."

He rises to his feet and pulls me up with him. "More than you know," he whispers.

thirty-six

I wait for one week, then a second. He has to grieve, to go over everything in his mind. I need to give him time, but I also need to see him. And there's still one thing that troubles me and I can't keep it inside me any longer.

We agree to meet at the beach one morning before he's on duty. The sky is overcast, and not many people are out.

Pilot can't seem to stand still. He's busy doing some kind of inventory of things around him, then going through the first-aid kit, checking supplies and finally waxing the surfboard with a strange surge of energy. I expect him to start vacuuming the sand next.

What I do know is that he'll never talk about our midnight ride and our time on the beach. That was some surreal experience for both of us. It brought us closer, but how close?

Right now he's very much back into form. The lifeguard, the healer, the guardian of other people's lives and fates.

"Can you stop...for just a minute?"

Annoyance creeps up my spine. I need to get his attention, for him to just focus on *me*, but maybe that's not fair. Now, with the tears behind him, Pilot's way of dealing with the loss is to keep in motion, as though constant activity will push the thoughts of Antonio away and ease the pain. Finally he stops and turns to me. He drops down next to me on the blanket. After gazing out at the ocean briefly, he turns to me and narrows his eyes.

"What...What is it?"

Now that I have his attention, I'm afraid to speak. I don't want it to come out wrong. I don't want to sound like a stupid, jealous, insecure baby, but I have to ask him. I have to know that the night out on the bike meant something real. I have to know that he wanted to be with *me*, not just have a warm body behind him when maybe Adriana wasn't there. I have to know that when he was at his lowest point he wanted *me* to be the one who tried to draw the sadness out of his heart with total surrender.

"It's about Adriana," I say, finally. I try to sneak in a breath without letting him know that what I'm about to ask him makes me need more oxygen. Maybe I'm prying into his private world, but I don't care anymore.

"Do you love her?"

He looks at me curiously. "Of course, why? Why are you asking me that?"

I swallow, involuntarily. His words sting. I feel like I've been slapped. "I see you with her so much...I had to know...I had to know that she really *is* your girlfriend."

"My *girlfriend*?"

"Jesus, Pilot, why are you making this even harder for me?"

"I've known Adriana since I was ten," he says, a flash of impatience in his voice. "She's lived with us for half my life."

"But you love her, you just said it."

"When I first met her, she was like a girlfriend, " he says, looking off. "Like a first love kind of thing." Then he shakes his head. "But after a year, maybe less, her mother was sick and she came to live with us." He runs a hand through his hair. "She became like a sister," he says. "It's been that way ever since."

I look back at him and can't help the smile that slowly spreads over my face.

"You were jealous?" he says, as if it is the most absurd thought. Then his face softens, enjoying this.

"Well..."

He tilts back his head and laughs.

Dear Marissa:

There are moments when I think I've totally lost it. There are things in front of me that I just don't understand for what they are. Pilot's "girlfriend," it turns out, is not his girlfriend. Adriana has lived with him and Antonio since he was ten. Yes, he loves her, but more like a sister. And Antonio, who left my day world and slipped into my dream world, was more like a grandfather to her.

As for me and Pilot... oh, there's so much to say and I have you see you in person to tell you.

But what I do see now is that Antonio left this world, but not without leaving me more than heartfelt memories. I paint with his brush now and ever since, something magical has happened on the canvas. I can capture changing light that I couldn't see before—the iridescent colors of flower petals in the sunlight, the luminous sheen of the ocean as it darkens at the end of the day. It just comes to me as if a window has opened up and for the first time what comes in are a radiant light and fresh, clean new air.

Is that something one person can leave to another? It doesn't seem possible. I'd be the first to deny it, but what other way is there to explain it? I'm dizzy with inspiration and I can't stop painting. Is that passion or madness? Is there a difference?.

I know you think I'm crazy. And as usual, you're right.

Can't wait to see you—and paint you!

My love,

Sirena

Sirena, my God, it seems like Antonio left you the ultimate gift, a paintbrush with a life and powers of its own! He must have loved you like one of his own children.

I laughed out loud when you told me about Adriana. How could you not tell they weren't romantically involved? You always did have a blind side. Anyway, I couldn't bear the thought of Pilot with another girl. You two seem destined to be together. I have to confess that I have a crush on him too. I love his looks and his mystery. He seems to exist on some other frequency. How could I not feel that way, after all you've told me about him? And that picture you sent. It seems alive!

Camp life is so completely dull and dismal compared to your world. We had the camp play. I got a great round of applause, blah, blah, blah. Geoff and I are totally over. He's intensely weird and isn't ready for a relationship, he says. I'm almost glad because I wouldn't want to be crazed about leaving him at the end of the summer if we had something serious going on. I am now so glad this will be my last summer stuck away in camp. I'm ready to work, I'm ready to do something else. How long can you spend rowing, making clay pots and having relay races? It's time for color wars to end and for real life to start, don't you think?

See you in less than a week!

Love,

Marissa

thirty-seven

The storm hits violently in the middle of the night. Crashing, deafening thunder, as if the tectonic plates of the earth are smashing each other in rage and the world is self-destructing. I'm glad. It expresses the torment inside me, the fury I feel toward a world that took Antonio from me. I feel cheated and hollow inside. He was my protector, my guiding light, my spiritual leader.

I looked up the word *shaman*. Its roots are in a Siberian language. It means a healer who sees in the dark. With my parents halfway across the country and Antonio gone, the whole world seems dark.

Quivering bolts of lightning break over the ocean like

ragged harpoons piercing the blackness. Rain hammers the windows. Will snuggles into my blanket, eyes wide. He doesn't like the noise, but he's not as phobic as some animals. I think of Edna, all alone now, without Antonio. Is she up now? What is she thinking? How much does that poor, wonderful dog understand? How does she go on? Pilot told me that she sleeps with him now. It's hard for her, he says, but he thinks she understands.

It hasn't stormed like this in weeks. I know what's ahead. I don't look forward to the attic.

"You can sleep downstairs?" Aunt Ellie says, without prompting.

"It's fine," I say, even though it's not. This isn't my first storm here. What will happen isn't new to me. It won't bother me as much if I act as if it's no big deal. I get into bed tucking the blanket around me like a protective shield, then close my eyes, ignoring everything outside.

This time when the whistling and moaning start, they're louder than I ever remember them. The keening builds to a hideous, unending screeching that gnaws through my bones and could shatter glass. The ghosts seem determined to be heard over the din outside. I cover my ears to block out the sound, but it's useless. The eerie shrieks come through on some other frequency, a pathway to the brain that can't be shut out with fingers pressed hard into my ears. I put my head under the blanket and hug Will, inhaling his furry warmth and doggy smell.

I lie back on the bed, a pillow the size of a body bag draped over my head. I feel my body giving way, sinking into sleep, when out of nowhere the air around me darkens to inky blackness. I squint and make out an unknowable shape looming over me. As it moves closer, I realize it's a stingray the size of the room. It unfurls its sluggish body only feet above me like a dark cape. It's larger than anything I've ever seen in nature before, as terrifying as the train-long anacondas of the Amazon that Antonio whispered about.

Like a heavy, smothering blanket of living flesh, the giant stingray blocks out all outside light. Slowly and steadily it lowers itself over me. I fixate on the razor sharp barb, a long lazy tail dragging behind it, narrow and out of proportion to its mass. Hard to imagine the deadly weapon it can become, lashing whiplike in self-defense in the face of threat, the serrated edge sharp as the jagged teeth of a carving knife. It floats nearer, the black, shining eyes, like marbles of anthracite, staring ahead, cold, emotionless, intent. It moves closer and closer and closer, choking off the air.

"No," I try to yell, only no sounds come out of my mouth. "Not again." My voice is trapped inside my body. I can't speak. I struggle like a mute, with the words stuck inside my throat. The silent screams echo inside me, my vocal cords getting raw from the futile effort. "Stop, stop, stop."

Frantically, I beg for help, for Pilot. Where is he? The massive creature is only inches away now, the eyes still staring, giving no hint of its plan or its motivation. I try to reach out to shove it away, but the effort is useless because its enormous weight and size are crushing down now and I can hardly breathe.

A tremendous crash outside makes me jump up, my T-shirt soaked with sweat, my heart ramming my chest. I run down the stairs to escape. Even with the storm, all I can think of is getting away from the house and getting outside, away from danger. The creaky stairs seem to scream and splinter as I bound down them. Crashes of thunder cover my sounds. The screen door slams behind me and I run toward the beach. It's black outside, no moonlight or stars to light the way. The wind is blowing hard, the rain pounding steadily in heavy sheets in every direction, its coolness washing away my sweat. Without warning, *swack*, something slams me hard from behind. I fall forward hitting the concrete, sprawling below my attacker.

"Help," I scream, "Help." But there's no one nearby to hear. I look all around, the rain pelting my face, but there's no one anywhere. What was that? Who did it? I search around frantically.

And then I see.

A thick tree branch. It's lying on the ground next to me. It hit like a flying missile. I rub the back of head and try to catch my breath; the sound of my frantic heart is strangely comforting. I'm alive, safe, outside, out of the ocean. Only a tree branch, nothing that will rear up and attack. I start running again, relief mixed with fear, confusion, and anxiety, my stride getting stronger and surer as I go. I have no idea where I'm headed or why I keep going, but I can't imagine slowing down or stopping. The ocean is as wild and as choppy as I've ever seen it. Waves smash against the shore again and again in a steady, jerky rhythm as if nature is vomiting water out of the ocean in massive spasms.

The fog is so thick that everything before me is indistinct, the world seen through a lens coated with Vaseline. A car drives by on the road, turning off and becoming an incandescent smear of light as it goes off into the distance. I make out a shining window of a house, an eerie, yellow glow in the blackness.

Then I slow down, exhausted.

A short distance in front of me, I make out the outline of a person. Or at least I think it is. He must be slumped down. I get closer and realize it's not a person at all. It's a black sack of garbage that must have blown from the front of someone's house. Am I hallucinating? I scold myself and keep going. A car whizzes by and slows down. Is it after me? Then it passes. The driver was only being cautious.

I'm at least half a mile from Aunt Ellie's house now. Where am I going? I can't stay out alone all night in this tempest. But I can't go back to the house, I can't, and nothing makes sense anymore. I hunker near a tree, wiping my eyes with the back of my hands, pushing the hair from my face. There's so much lightning and thunder. I shouldn't be here. I shouldn't be outside. I should be low to the ground. I turn and start to run home.

Only something or someone is in my path.

I stop.

Alone? He seems to be. Lost too? I run toward him and then slow down.

What am I seeing? It's the dark of night in the fury of a storm. Why would anyone be on the beach? Why would anyone, except me, escape *into* a storm to get away from a house of ghosts and ghastly sounds, grotesque memories of things that happened that I still don't understand and maybe no one living does or ever will.

I slow to a stop, the rain pelting my face so hard that I have to keep pushing my dripping hair away to see clearly. And then I do.

Pilot.

There's a glow around him, an incandescent arc. Rain washes down over the planes of his strong, angular face. His white T-shirt clings to the sharp outlines of his chest. There's no surprise in his eyes when he sees me. He looks at me as if he knew I'd come. It was just a matter of time.

His lips curl up into a small smile. "Sirena," he whispers, drawing me close to him. He doesn't ask why I'm there, he knows. Despite the cold rain, his body is warm and comforting. I breathe in the warm, sweet perfume of his neck and rest my head against it. He smoothes my hair back off my face.

I had to get away from the house...the ghosts..."

"I know," he whispers. "I know."

He takes my hand and leads me to the far end of the beach to the parking lot. His car is there and we climb inside. There are towels on the back seat and he opens one and dries my face and hair. He wraps it around my shoulders. It's warm and soft.

"Hold me." He puts his arms around me tightly and we sit there together, listening to the wind howling, rocking the car. I lose track of time. All at once I feel whole. I belong here. Pilot loosens his arms and looks into my face.

"I have to explain," he says. "I have so much to tell you."

"About what?"

"Let's get out of this," he says. He starts the engine and pulls away. The roads are flooded and slick. It's not safe to be out; it's not safe to drive.

"It's impossible to see," I whisper.

He looks over at me and smiles. His eyes burn green-gold in the dark.

He navigates easily circling around garbage strewn on the streets and tangles of fallen tree limbs. The car hugs the road as if it's programmed to get us where we're going safely. He pulls into the driveway at the side of a bright yellow-and-blue house at the end of what looks like a dead-end street. There's a light burning on the porch. It's a small bungalow, like an artist's retreat. I know I've never seen it before.

"Home," he says, reading my confusion.

He turns the doorknob of an unlocked yellow door and I follow him in. It's dark and warm. A dog barks and feet scurry toward us. Pilot turns on a lamp and Edna comes to us, wagging her tail. I kneel down and kiss her, running my hands over her dark, slick coat. She recognizes me, I can tell.

When I get to my feet and look around, the world has been transformed. I'm inside the rainforest and it's close to paradise. The walls are covered with giant canvases—Antonio's paintings of the Amazon jungle. I see muddy pathways surrounded by canopies of enormous trees. There are jaguars, snakes, and animals that don't look like animals, but more like spirits with glowing red eyes that peer out of hiding places in the trees, or lurk on the surface of the dark river. There are butterflies and orchids and all kinds of tropical flowers—hibiscus, frangipani, and giant water lilies along the bank of the river. I can almost hear the jungle sounds.

"Incredible."

"I wanted you to see it," Pilot says. "This was his world, the one he grew up in. Can you imagine?"

I stare at the canvases, hypnotized. They pulse with life.

"These were never in the gallery," he says. "He would never sell them. They made him feel at home."

"He told me so much about Brazil, but I never knew. I never knew he painted it."

"There's something else," Pilot says. "Close your eyes and don't open them until I tell you." He takes my hand and leads me into another room. We stop. He lets go of my hand and I hear him turn on a lamp.

"Now look."

I'm staring at a giant canvas of...myself. I swallow hard. "When...When did he do it?"

"It was his last painting. He planned to show it to you before..." His voice cracks.

I step toward it and stare, overcome with the oddest feeling. I'm looking at a reflection of myself in a mirror and my soul is reflected back to me. I'm sitting on the beach staring out at the water. My eyes are filled with a mixture of sadness, longing...and determination.

"What do you think?" Pilot says.

"I never posed for him; he never had a picture of me, yet everything, everything he knew about me ... it's all there."

"He *had* a picture, Sirena. You were in his heart."

We're standing in a bedroom. "This is my room," he says. He goes to the window and opens it. The rain is stopping and a cool breeze blows the gauzy white curtains up over his head. He stands at the window, profiled in the light from the outside.

"I have so much to tell you," he says. "There's so much you have to know. But it's so late now and you're tired." He looks at his watch. "I'll take you home. We can talk tomorrow."

I walk to the window and bury my face in his chest. "I don't want to go home."

He slides his hand down along the length of my arm and closes his hand over mine.

⸻

Aunt Ellie had an appointment with her editor. She left the morning of the storm and promised to be back the next day.

She'd never know I didn't come home.

⸻

Pilot buys orange juice and cinnamon muffins in a bakery on Main Street. He doesn't have to work until eleven. We eat breakfast on the beach in the early morning sunlight.

"These are like cake," he laughs, cinnamon powder

coating his lips. "Tonio used to love them."

We eat silently and finally he turns to me. "Just before he died, Tonio told me what happened to my mother. I always thought she got sick and died when I was ten, but that wasn't what happened. He said she was killed by the sword of a stingray." He looks into my eyes, studying the effects of his words. "She was diving for spider shells in the Caribbean. She must have struck it," he says, "just like what happened to you. But no one knows for sure."

"Why didn't he tell you before?"

"That's what I asked him. All he said was that it wasn't the time."

"Was she alone?"

"She was *with* Tonio, that's why he was so tormented. He taught her all about the ocean. She was swimming from the age of three. She loved the water more than anything. It just happened so fast." He stops, staring off. "He blamed himself all these years. He should have seen it, he thought. He should have prevented it."

"What about your father?"

"He didn't go with them that day. He never got over it..."

"And my dream...I don't understand..."

"They lived in your house a long time ago," he says. "The ghosts are the sounds of Antonio's wife, my grandmother, crying out for her daughter."

"But why only when it storms?"

"There was a terrible storm the day after it happened," he says. "As if the earth were venting its fury."

"But now...the stingray...I thought they didn't come here."

"They don't," he says. "But it followed him. Like evil always follows us." He touches my face and leans close to me. "When you were attacked, we both thought the same thing was about to happen. Somehow, despite our powers to heal, we didn't see it coming, we didn't expect it. Evil was stronger than we were. We were terrified you would die."

"But I didn't. You saved me, both of you."

"Yes, but the effort was too much for him. He was so depleted by then, he had given so much blood to you. He had already lost one child; he couldn't bear the thought of losing you too." He hesitates as though he's holding back. "You reminded him so much of her."

I shake my head. It was all too much. I realize I didn't understand anything. I look off, remembering all the things I said to Antonio.

"Antonio saw into me. He saw everything." My eyes fill with tears. "And he left me with so much of him," I whisper. "His gift for painting. His..." I struggle to find the right word. "His soul."

"My mother was a painter too," he says. "He kept the gift alive in you."

"I wish I could have his other gifts. The way he knows things and heals—the way you do too."

"How do you know you can't?"

"What?" I shake my head, not understanding.

"It was in his blood," he says. "Now it's in yours."

The heat of the sun bakes down on us. I move closer into him and he puts his arms around me. There's a sureness in me I've never felt before, a forcefulness that fills every cell, magnifying who I am, expanding my consciousness into a wider world outside of the physical reality of being on the beach, near the water. He presses his lips to the back of my neck and we fuse into one again. I turn to him, running my fingertips over his lips. They're hot, as hot as a flame. And now, so are mine.

thirty-eight

I zip my suitcase then take one long, last view out the bay window at the glittering ocean panorama. I snap one picture with my camera, then another. Finally, I close the shutters and turn my back on my oceanic room and the ghosts of history that will forever haunt its walls.

Will follows me down the stairs, his alert eyes taking in my every move. He knows this is a different day from the ones that came before. My doggy detective doesn't miss anything. He understands the language of suitcases and change. I kneel down and kiss his open, alert ears. "I'll be back," I whisper. Aunt Ellie opens her arms to give me a hug.

"Come visit next summer," she says. I nod, afraid if I speak my voice will betray me. When I arrived she was almost a stranger. Two months later, she became my second mom.

Nervously, I reach my hand into the pocket of my sweatshirt. I feel something that I think, at first, is a coin. But it isn't.

It's the charm on the now-broken chain from Louisiana that Marissa gave me before I left. I look at it again.

"Arrive the same, leave different," it says.

I walk outside to the car and Will darts out the door behind me. Pilot waits behind the wheel, tapping his hand against it. He stops when he sees me. Will leaps up and tries to jump through the open window. Pilot smiles and lifts him up. He gets out of the car and carries him back inside.

The sky is dark and overcast. Poetic justice. In six hours Rhode Island will be far behind me, a distant planet.

⸻

I press my head back against the seat as the plane goes faster and faster until it lifts off the ground. The ocean, so vast and glittering, gets farther and farther away until it's hidden behind masses of white mist, like mosquito netting forming a protective web around us. I close my hand around the two figas on my neck. The first from Antonio. The second, as blue-green as the ocean, from Pilot.

"Stay safe for me," he said, placing it around my neck as he kissed me for the last time.

Something from him to hold onto, to keep close to my heart. A lifeline between us until I saw him again.

Can you hear the way my heart is pounding now, even when I'm miles away from you?

We didn't talk much on the way to the airport. I didn't want to fill our last minutes together with white noise. Pilot looked over at me and smiled, then turned back to the road. I reached out and ran my fingers over the smooth, round curves of his hard shoulder, trying to make my fingers memorize the feel of his skin. Would I ever get over the need to steal glances at him, to drink him in? Would I ever feel I'd taken in enough of his face? His being? His touch?

His existence was my oxygen. I needed it to stay alive.

But right then I was inhaling hard, short breaths, trying to satisfy my burning, aching lungs. How could I bear the hurt? Like a sensitive barometer, he turned to me, narrowing his eyes.

"You okay?"

I nodded. "Fine." And then the tears came.

"I'll visit you at Christmas," he said. "Seeing you will be my present."

I promised to fly up to the University of Rhode Island at Easter. He has two more years before starting their graduate school of oceanography. So fitting that he'll devote his life to studying the ocean, a high priest in his temple.

For now I try to live in the moment. I focus on what's imminent. I'm going home to two new places to live. You don't ever get comfortable with the idea of your parents splitting apart, but it's been two months now and some of the sting is gone.

"You're your own person," Pilot said to me, the night of the storm. "You have to make your own way in the world."

"But my parents—"

"You have two of them," he says, resolutely.

I stop and catch myself.

"You're a survivor," he says. "Hold your head up and don't forget that."

⌘

So I draw strength from Pilot and from Antonio, my guardian angels. I turn inward and tap into the power I have to heal myself and make the most of my life. I still have two parents, even if they're not together. I try not to blame them anymore. There's no point to that.

"Our marriage didn't fail," my mom says. "But it's like a living thing and it's changeable and unpredictable."

"But Dad—"

"Things happen for a reason," she says, and stops. I don't need to know everything. What I do know is that relationships aren't simple. And not always the way they appear.

"Both of us will try harder than before to be there for you," she says. "You've lost a house, but you haven't lost me—or your dad."

I'll miss the house where I grew up, and especially the big oak tree outside. For as long as I can remember, the

273

old tree with its strong, gnarled arms spread wide open has been standing sentry in our front yard. But one day while I was away, there was a bad storm, my mom said. She heard a deafening boom outside and she ran to the window.

"The tree was struck by lightning," she said.

I look at the black burn mark now, a painful scar all across its trunk. It hurts me to look at it.

"Let's watch it, give it time," the arborist said. "We'll see if it makes it."

I can't think that it might not.

Weeks after we move out of the house, I drive by just to see it again. I stop just short of the driveway. There are different bushes outside now and new flowers. The old oak tree is still there though, and the black burn mark still scars its thick trunk. Only now there are bright green shoots coming out of the sides of the trunk.

Something else unexpected turned out for me after I returned to Texas, something I never counted on at all or could have imagined.

The phone rang one night when my mom and I were in the middle of dinner. I jumped up and grabbed it.

"Will is so sad without you," Aunt Ellie said. "He still sleeps in your bed, and he mopes around the house like a lost soul." She puts the phone to his ear and I speak to him.

"His face lit up," she shouts, laughing. She asks to speak to my mom and I watch her face as she talks to Aunt Ellie.

"I don't know," she says warily. She listens some more and nods, almost to herself. A few "uh huhs," and then silence. Then she holds the phone away and turns to me.

"Ellie said the house is getting filled up because while Pilot and Adriana are in school, she's taking care of Edna, so she'd be willing to drive Will down here...and if he's happy here and you want him, she said you could keep him."

"Are you kidding? YES," I scream into the phone. "YES!"

So Will and I will have two homes and he'll have a bed and dog dishes in each one of them. He won't have the beach anymore, but he'll have two backyards instead of one. He may be confused at first. He may miss losing the first home he had, but in the long run, learning to cope with change can make you stronger.

"Children have energy, strong spirits, great resources," Antonio said. "Nature wants them to survive."

He might have been thinking about Will too.

And also about me.

⸺◦◦◦⸺

I'm up in my room in my mom's new house when the phone rings one night.

Pilot.

I know his phone number by heart.

"Sirena," he says. Just my name. But in a microsecond,

the sound of his soft, easy voice is all it takes to bring me back to one special moment when we were together. I had just come out of the ocean and was standing on my blanket on the beach in the hot sun. I turned to face him, to take him in, while he stared nakedly at me through his binoculars and the outside world seemed to fall away, leaving just the two of us in the universe. He's two thousand miles away now, but I can see his face as clearly and feel his presence around me.

"There's a full moon tonight," he says. "I can't stop thinking about you."

I go to the window and stare out at it. "I can see it from my room."

"I know you can."

"How do you know that?" I say, sitting on the edge of my bed.

"I saw you in a dream."

"What did you see?"

"You were home. You were painting."

I stare across the room at the easel. There's a canvas on it. I started a picture, but it's unfinished.

"What's on the canvas?" I ask him. My heart starts to pound.

He laughs softly. "A picture of me."

I've done more than ten of them, I'm obsessed. If I tell him, he'll think I'm crazy.

"You're scaring me. You know too much."

He laughs. "I can't help it." Then he's silent. I hear him exhale. "I miss you," he says, his voice turning serious.

"I miss you too."

My heart starts to thump in my chest. Can he hear it when we're so far apart?

"Yes," he says. "I can."